WATCHING WILLOW

THE GOLD COAST RETRIEVERS

ANN OMASTA

FREE BOOK!

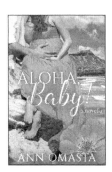

Escape to the enchanting Hawaiian Islands in Leilani's heartwarming tale of friendship, love, and triumph after heartbreak.

Visit annomasta.com and tell us where to send your free novella. You can unsubscribe at any time.

*W*illow Winks stared at her reflection in her dressing room's brightly-lit magnifying mirror. She slowly turned her face from side to side, inspecting for flaws. Sighing with disgust, she flicked off the harsh lights. A few wrinkles, thinning hair, and a slightly sagging jaw weren't valid reasons to be demoted, or possibly fired--*were they?*

Unfortunately, in her profession, she feared that was exactly what would happen. For a woman on television, looks were everything. Unfortunately for her, the studio would look for the first viable excuse to get rid of an aging female talk show host.

Of course, they would never admit she was being cut loose due to her age. The optics and liability of being sued would force them to avoid admitting that as the reason for her dismissal. Declining ratings would be pointed out as the rationale. They would have colorful graphs and complicated charts to back-up the decision, but it would still boil down to the same thing... No one wanted to watch a woman age, no matter how gracefully she attempted to do so.

She could use injections and minor procedures in a vain attempt to hold off the inevitable, but they could only do so much. Besides, there were plenty of examples of people going too far with these quick-fixes and ending up looking like frightening, taut versions of their former selves. The last thing she wanted was to look perpetually surprised because her skin was pulled back too tight.

Deciding that she couldn't put off the inevitable any longer, she took a deep breath and headed out the door of her dressing room.

On the way to the elevator, she passed by a trio of teenaged girls. She assumed they were backstage in hopes of seeing Dash Diamond and Star, the successful duo who co-hosted *Good Morning Gold Coast,* a live morning program that aired just before Willow's show each weekday morning.

When the girls beamed at her, their eyes sparkling with recognition, Willow paused. "Hi," she greeted them, giving them the option to speak to her, if they wished.

Her carefully practiced voice no longer held even a trace of her Southern drawl. The studio had insisted upon her arrival that she take voice lessons to get rid of any hint of twang. Even though her family had balked and insisted that it was one of the things that made her stand out in a sea of hopeful starlets, her Georgia accent had been systematically eliminated from her speech years ago.

Three sets of eyes gawked back at her, wide-open and, Willow hoped, star-struck. "Aren't you ladies supposed to be in school?" She lightly chastised them, but smiled to let them know she was just teasing.

When one of the girls lifted the latest iPhone model and pointed it in Willow's direction, Willow quickly offered, "How about a selfie?"

All three nodded, so Willow took the phone, turned and encouraged all three girls to look up at the camera. Willow knew her best angles from years of experience, so she always commandeered the phones from her fans to make sure there wasn't an unflattering picture of her floating around online. She gave one of her practiced smiles and snapped the shot.

The girls nodded and thanked her profusely, after suddenly finding their voices. Willow handed the phone back and patted the closest girl on the back as she eased past them in the hallway.

It had been a great interaction, even if the girls had been hoping for a glimpse of handsome Dash Diamond. Often, people forgot she was a real person with genuine feelings. It wasn't unusual for someone to tell her that she looked better in person or on television. Both sentiments left her feeling worse after hearing them. She wanted to look good for her job, but no one wanted to be told they didn't look great in real life.

Still smiling, she continued her trek to the elevator en route to her meeting with the studio bigwigs upstairs. They had unceremoniously summoned her without so much as a hint as to what they wanted. The mysterious mandatory get-together was nerve wracking.

She almost didn't notice the mousy woman standing near the elevator holding some printed photos of Dash and Star, his four-legged companion. When the woman started rifling through the stack and muttering to herself, Willow smiled and reached around her to push the up button to call the elevator.

Obviously pleased to have found one, the woman's face lit up when she pulled out a dated photo of Willow. She presented it and a black Sharpie marker to Willow for an autograph.

It normally annoyed Willow when people shoved photos into her face without even bothering to speak to her. Since this woman had been allowed past security and into the studio, Willow assumed that she must know someone, so she made a snap decision to break her own rule and sign the picture.

Glancing down, she realized the shot was from her early days when she first started hosting the show. The lovely, fresh-faced girl smiling up at her from the photo made Willow's perfectly arched eyebrows furrow together. With this photo evidence, it was impossible to pretend that her face hadn't aged much over the years.

As she stared at the picture, holding the Sharpie just over it, the woman tapped her foot impatiently. "Just sign it," she finally ordered Willow.

Taken aback by the abrupt woman's rudeness, Willow's head snapped up just in time to see Dash

Diamond and Star emerge from their dressing room. The woman saw them too and chose to snatch the marker and unsigned picture back from Willow. "Just forget it. Your signature won't sell for much anyway."

With those cutting words, the woman ran up to Dash and Star, leaving Willow feeling even more self-conscious and past her prime.

Blinking back the burning tears and refusing to let them fall, Willow took a calming breath and punched the button on the elevator to head up to the top floor to face her fate.

$\mathcal{W}$illow's eyelashes fluttered as she blinked rapidly and made a valiant attempt not to cry. The studio's head honcho was staring at her unflinchingly from his place of honor at the head of the large mahogany conference room table. The other executives seated around the shiny oval table looked down or stared just past her, refusing or unable to make eye contact with her.

Even though she had believed herself to be mentally prepared for this, it still came as a shock. Reminding herself that it wasn't as bad as it could be, she straightened her spine and focused on keeping her voice from squeaking when she asked, "So, I'm being demoted?"

"Don't look at it as a demotion." Her boss tried to placate her, but failed miserably.

Channeling her hurt feelings into anger, Willow glared back at him, practically daring him to object. "How else could I look at it? Are you trying to insinuate that going from hosting an hour-long live show to being a cheesy host on a half-hour recorded game show isn't a demotion?"

"Let's look at it as more of a lateral move." He smiled, revealing his bridged, perfect teeth.

"There's nothing lateral about this move, and we all know it." She looked around at each set of eyes in the room. Willow had been here when most of these men and women started working at the studio. She considered many of them to be friends outside of the office, yet no one was willing to stand up for her in this pivotal moment in her career.

Deciding to call them out on what she knew to be the ugly truth, she accused, "This is because I'm getting older."

"That has nothing to do with it." Her boss immediately backpedaled, knowing that the legal department would have a fit if he admitted to ageism. Ruffling through his file of papers, he pulled out a graph depicting a declining trend line.

Giving her a stern stare, he said, "The numbers don't lie."

Willow felt like she had been punched in the gut. "The numbers can be manipulated," she accused, even though she knew her ratings had been in a prolonged slump.

Feeling backed into a corner, she played the only other card she could think of. "Is this because I'm a female? I notice that Dash Diamond isn't in here losing his show."

She knew she was pushing the boundaries of propriety, but she was desperate to cling to the job that defined her. Without her status as a local

8

celebrity, she was nothing. When her boss pulled a second sheet out of his file folder, one glance at the upward trend made her shoulders fold inward.

"I had the feeling you might say that, so I printed out a copy of Dash and Star's numbers. See the difference?" He asked with unnecessary venom in his tone.

He seemed to be waiting for an answer, so Willow nodded, feeling properly chastised.

Leaning forward and pressing his palms together, the studio's CEO told Willow, "We are all rooting for you. In fact, these numbers indicate that you should be fired, but we aren't quite ready to go to that extreme."

Willow's breath sucked in involuntarily at this revelation. She could feel the blood rushing out of her head as a wave of nausea overwhelmed her. It dawned on her then that building her whole life around her career had been a monumental mistake. Something that can be taken away so swiftly and easily was clearly the wrong thing to base her sense of self-worth on.

Trying, but failing, to appear on her side, her boss splayed his hands to indicate the others in the room as he continued, "We don't want to lose you, Willow. That's why we are offering you this last chance to redeem yourself." Looking down his glasses at her, he added solemnly, "You need to take it and be grateful for it. I strongly suggest you find a way to make it work."

His thinly-veiled threat wasn't lost on Willow. It was obvious that if the numbers for the game show weren't impressive, she would be kicked to the curb. Nodding to acknowledge her understanding, Willow pushed back from the massive table. "Is that all?"

At his confirming nod, she ran out of the room with her palm over her mouth. Silently amending her previous thought, she decided the only thing worse than being an aging local celebrity is being an aging local celebrity that no one wants.

3

*S*itting alone in her dressing room only made Willow want to throw something. She was rational enough to know that wouldn't help anything, so she decided she needed to talk to someone. There was only one person in the entire building who had a sliver of a chance of understanding what she was going through, so she headed down the hallway to knock on Dash Diamond's door.

She was a little surprised when he flung the door open, since he wasn't known for sticking around long after his show. His face lit up with surprise when he saw Willow on the other side.

"Come in!" He offered enthusiastically. He had no doubt thought the visitor was someone who wanted something from him.

It had been a long time since Willow had reached out to Dash, so she was thrilled to see his warm expression. The two of them had started at the studio within months of each other, both thrust into local stardom with very little preparation. They had even tried a short-lived romance, but they quickly discovered that there is only room for one diva in a relationship.

Star's fluffy tail wagged excitedly to welcome Willow into the room.

"I hope I'm not bothering you." Willow gave Dash an out, in case he had another commitment.

"Not at all," he assured her. "Star and I were just working on a few new tricks."

Turning to address the dog, he added, "Weren't we, sweet girl?"

Willow frowned, but tried to hide her shock over him talking to the dog as if she could understand him. Deciding that maybe the fame had gotten to him more than she knew, she shook her head to clear it and said, "I could really use a friend right now."

"Of course," Dash searched her face as he indicated for her to sit down on his luxurious leather sofa.

Accepting the offered seat allowed her a perfect view out the picture window, which looked out over the coastline. Swallowing her jealousy over his primo view, she admitted quietly, "I just got demoted."

Obviously stunned, Dash's mouth hung open after he said, "What??"

Willow nodded to confirm, but they sat in silence for a long moment. It was unheard of for Dash Diamond, the consummate talk-show host, to be silent for this long, so Willow felt sure that her announcement had been news to him.

Relief surged through her that she evidently

wasn't the laughing stock of the entire studio. If Dash hadn't caught wind of her fledgling ratings, then it clearly wasn't as widespread as she had feared.

Since Dash had added his golden retriever co-host, Star, to his show and met Grace, the love of his life, he had become the undeniable heart of the entire studio. His newfound zest for life made him universally beloved, and he had his finger on the pulse of the goings-on at their network's head-quarters.

Taking a deep breath to steel her resolve, Willow launched into the brutal truth. "My ratings have been taking a nosedive for months... well, years," she admitted with a self-effacing, sad chuckle.

"We'll think of a way to revive them," Dash promised her fervently.

She smiled, valuing the man's friendship. "It's too late for that," she told him solemnly. "The good news is that they aren't firing me... yet."

She let the threat hanging over her head dangle between them for a long moment. "My show has been cancelled."

Dash's quick intake of breath made her smile. She had known he would be one of the few who could truly understand her predicament. Quickly going on she added, "They are giving me a match-making game show instead."

"Oh," Dash said, running his fingers through his thick hair as he processed her revelation. Trying to put a positive spin on it, he said, "That's great. You'll be fantastic at that."

She appreciated his valiant effort to be

supportive, but they both knew this wasn't good news. Calling him out on it, she said, "They have the door open and are rearing back to kick me out, and we both know it."

Nodding, Dash acknowledged that her position at the studio was precarious. After thinking about it for a long moment, he said, "Well, we will just have to make sure your new show is a smashing success."

"And how exactly would you suggest I do that?" She gave him a sad smile, pleased that he was willing to help, but confident that she was in an impossible situation.

"I'm not sure, but we'll think of something." Dash promised her sincerely.

They sat in silence for a long, serious moment. It wasn't until Star gave them a firm, demanding "Woof!" that they looked at each other with their eyes alight with renewed hope.

4

*S*tanding and pacing to the other side of the room, Willow said, "Just because it renewed your show doesn't mean the dog gimmick will work to make my new show's ratings soar."

"Star is hardly a gimmick." Dash immediately jumped to his beloved dog's defense. Softening his facial features as he gazed down at his pet, he added, "The audience loves her, and she enhances my show in ways that I never imagined to be possible."

"It's easy to see that you love your dog." Willow smiled as she watched him absently rub his large hand over Star's dome-shaped furry head.

Star closed her chocolate-brown eyes and pressed her head up into Dash's loving palm.

"I've never been a dog person." Willow admitted as she crinkled her nose and thought about shedding, fleas, noxious odors, and muddy paws.

"Believe it or not, I wasn't either," Dash shook his head as if he couldn't quite comprehend it either. "Somehow a special dog can wiggle its way right into your heart."

Willow nodded. She had always marveled at how Star had transformed Dash's show and life--especially considering how much the man had fought bonding with the dog. It was obvious to anyone who spent more than a few moments with them that the man was completely smitten by the animal, and the feeling was obviously mutual.

"If a dog can make my game show have even a fraction of the success that your show has enjoyed, then it is worth it to deal with an animal invading my space." Willow decided aloud.

Dash's blue eyes darkened. In a serious tone he said, "You know, there is more to life than ratings, wealth, and fame."

"There is?" She asked, pretending to be stunned by this revelation. Even though she was joking, she knew that she didn't actually have much else in her life besides her career. The lack of any other focus made her demotion seem like even more of a crushing blow.

Dash had a flourishing career and a rewarding personal life, so it was easy for him to be flippant about it. She had always felt like she needed to choose one or the other, and she had consistently opted for work. For the first time since moving to California, she was beginning to wonder if that laser focus had been a mistake.

Dash smiled sadly at her lame joke. It was obvious that he was well aware that having a successful career had been her only goal for far too long. Seeming to make a decision, he said, "It's worth a shot. Besides, you might be surprised how much joy a dog will bring into your life."

"Right," she nodded, even though it was obvious by her flat tone that she didn't believe him.

"You'll see," Dash told her, sounding supremely confident. His eyes lit up with a teasing expression right before he added, "A dog might even be able to melt the ice around that cold, vain heart of yours."

Accepting his ribbing good-naturedly, she stood to leave and said, "Worked for yours, right?"

Dash laughed, enjoying their easy banter together. When she reached the door and turned back, he turned serious again. "I'll send you the contact information for Carol Graves, the breeder where we got Star. She's reputable and kindhearted."

After a moment of silence where they both seemed deep in thought, Dash added, "She'll help you. I think you'll find that the right dog will change your life for the better in ways that you can't even imagine."

Holding up her crossed fingers, Willow said, "Let's hope," before heading out into the hallway feeling renewed hope that this downturn might not be as bad as she feared.

At a loss for anything else to do, she texted her driver, Nico, to request that he bring the car to the front of the studio to pick her up. It was time for her to return to her huge, empty house––alone, as usual.

5

*W*illow kept busy by doing a yoga session with her personal trainer, having her masseuse drive over for a ninety-minute session to work out the tight kinks in her shoulders, and requesting her chef to make chicken stir-fry for dinner. It wasn't lost on her that, other than people she paid, there wasn't anyone outside of work in her daily life.

No one chose to spend time with her. If she lost her job, it wouldn't be long until she could no longer afford to hire people to hang out with her. She would probably become one of those hermit recluses, who died alone and wasn't found for weeks.

The very real possibility chilled her to the bone. She shivered and shook her head, trying to rid that horrifying mental image from her mind.

When Dash texted the contact information for Carol Graves, she stared at the number for a long moment. She wasn't sure about taking on the responsibility of another living being's life.

Deciding she could hire a dog walker, a trainer, and anything else the animal needed, she punched the button to dial Carol's number before she could chicken out. They scheduled a time for Willow to go to Carol's house later that evening.

As Willow disconnected the call, she tried to tell herself she could just go look at the latest litter of golden pups Carol had raved about on the phone. Nothing said she had to take one home with her. *Famous last words...* She rolled her eyes, knowing that she wouldn't be able to resist bringing a new friend home with her.

Now that she had warmed to the idea, she was excited to put her plan into action. The time waiting to go to Carol's house seemed to drag on interminably. Willow's life felt especially empty now that it had been painfully pointed out to her that the one thing she had going for her could easily disappear in an instant.

She prattled around the big oceanfront house that was situated adjacent to Redwood Cove's famous, picturesque cliff walk. She had people to cook and clean for her, she was driven around and pampered by others. All of her helpers made it so she didn't have to do anything for herself, which left her at a loss for something to occupy her free time. Normally, she sat down to watch television--convincing herself it was research for her show--but her heart just wasn't in it today.

An hour before her scheduled time to meet Carol at her house, Willow searched her massive closet for something appropriate to wear to meet puppies. She inherently knew that jeans would be the best choice, but she didn't have many of those in her wardrobe.

Generally, she wore the fancy designer clothes the show provided to her, or when she was home, she opted for Lululemon stretchy black pants that she could pair with anything from a fitted tee-shirt to a silky button-up blouse.

Walking to the back of her massive closet, she gazed at the only two pairs of jeans she had left-over from her previous life. They were neatly pressed and hanging along the back wall of her closet. Of course, the style of them was horribly dated now, but she still ran her hand along the soft denim fabric.

She wasn't sure what sick compulsion had made her keep the too-tight pants all this time. Perhaps they were a cruel reminder of how her judgmental mother could make her feel inade-quate with one simple, cutting statement.

The first time she remembered her mother insinuating she needed to lose weight was when she was the fragile, formative age of twelve. Her mother had looked her over from head to toe before pronouncing that Willow's choice of pants made her butt look flabby.

That hurtful comment had set Willow up for a lifetime of watching every bite that went into her mouth, counting calories, and praying that she wouldn't gain any weight. From that point on, her mother made it a point to comment any time Willow ate something unhealthy or didn't get enough exercise for the day.

Looking back on it now, Willow realized that

her mother's judgment was likely a big reason why Willow felt the need to escape to California as soon as she graduated high school to pursue a career in show business. Of course, escaping that one woman's judgment had thrown her straight into the frying pan of the public's harsh opinions.

An online witch-hunt had formed a few years ago when Willow wore a shirt on air that was a tad too tight. Words like "fat cow" and "obese" had been thrown around online as if she weren't a real person with feelings. She had vowed then never to look at unfiltered online comments again. Now, she had Evelyn, a production assistant at the office, sift through them and only show her the positive ones. Willow's fragile ego couldn't handle the full brunt of the internet bullies, who liked to hide behind their screen names.

She considered for at least the thousandth time getting rid of her old blue jeans. Deciding they would make good 'flu pants' for if she was sick or lost a few pounds after a juice cleanse, she ignored the mental nudge that it might be time to get rid of the dated denim.

Besides, they might come back into style soon, right? These types of things always seemed to roll in twenty-year cycles, so they were due for a comeback. She couldn't keep the hope at bay that they might actually fit when their time came back around. Apparently, old habits died very hard.

It wasn't that she was overweight, and she knew that. But there always seemed to be that extra seven pounds that she couldn't quite get rid of, no matter how hard she tried. She guessed it was just the bane of being a woman of a certain age. Men never seemed to struggle with such problems. Even if they did carry a little extra weight, it didn't appear to bother them like it did females. *Sigh.*

Smiling to herself, Willow decided that at least if her judgmental mother ever said anything nice to her, she would know it was sincere. She'd been waiting a long time for that to happen, but maybe one of these days it would.

Knowing she needed a mental shift, she scraped hangers along the bar to hide her jeans in the back of the closet where they belonged. She still had on black pants from yoga, so she selected a black and white silk shirt to go with them. She silently hoped that the little buggers wouldn't get light-colored fur all over her, but decided that the potential for finding a lifelong friend, like Star was to Dash, was worth the risk.

After donning some bedazzled, sparkling black and silver tennis shoes, she proclaimed herself to be ready to meet the dog that would hopefully save her job––and quite possibly her life.

6

*O*n the ride over to Carol's house, Willow tried not to get her hopes up too high. She knew what it was like to have a mother who expected too much, and she didn't want to do that to anyone––not even a dog. That fear that she might be too much like her own mother was the main reason Willow had never had children. Well, that and the fact that she hadn't met a man who seemed like appropriate father material.

Most of the men in her life were focused mostly on money and getting more of it. That greedy lifestyle didn't exactly make her confident in their potential paternal skills.

Deciding it was her own fault for always going for the wrong kind of guy, she looked out the car's back window as the picturesque scenery blurred past. Since Nico was her regular driver, he knew that she liked to take the coastal route, unless it was completely in the wrong direction.

Since she had grown up in the middle of Georgia, the ocean view was something she truly appreciated. That was one thing that she hadn't become jaded about during her time in California. Looking at the water still mesmerized her. She could gaze at it for hours, wondering what beautiful creatures were swimming in its depths or just below the surface.

Nico had found a route to Carol's that let Willow enjoy the ocean view, so she tried to relax back into the plush leather seat. The niggling fear that she wouldn't find a puppy or worse, that the puppy she chose wouldn't like her, refused to completely abate, despite the lovely scenery sweeping past her window. The last thing she wanted was to be the one person that a loving and sweet golden retriever didn't like.

Making a snap decision, Willow determined that she would choose a male puppy. That would make it seem less like she was copying Dash and Star's shtick, plus it would give her a man in her life.

Shaking her head in disgust that this is what her life had become, she pictured herself naming the dog a masculine, human-sounding name, like Jake. She could then tell her mother on their weekly phone calls all about her fun adventures with Jake. Since her mother had no desire to visit California, and her father refused to travel out of state, Willow could safely use that to get her mother off her back about finding a husband. Handsome, sweet, and doting Jake could be the answer to her prayers.

When the car stopped at Carol's address, Willow swiped her sweaty palms along her stretchy cotton pants. There was no denying her nerves had kicked into high gear. She felt like she was going for a job interview, even though she knew it was silly.

After Nico circled the car and opened her door, she was tempted to ask the driver to come inside with her, but she knew that was beyond the bounds of his job description. It's not like they were friends. He was just someone whom she hired to spend time with her, just like almost everyone else in her life.

Walking up the sidewalk, Willow balled her fists in an effort not to wring her hands nervously. Telling herself it was silly to be so nervous about meeting a puppy, she punched the button for the doorbell.

When Carol opened the door, Willow was pleased to see that the woman had a kind, gentle face. Just as Willow was wondering if they might be able to become friends, Carol stared at her a moment too long in a way that Willow was familiar with. It was obvious by that stare that Carol recognized her from the show.

Sighing, Willow realized that spark of recognition would pretty much ruin her chance of forging a friendship with the other woman. For some reason, her being a celebrity caused other people to put her on a pedestal that was hard to live up to in real life. Instead, she ended up avoiding interacting with them on a deeper level to keep from disappointing them.

Willow introduced herself, even though it was obvious that Carol knew who she was. When they lightly shook hands, Willow realized that Carol's hands were damp too. They were evidently both nervous about this meeting.

"Come in," Carol offered politely.

A beautiful dog with a shiny reddish coat came to greet Willow. He nudged his head into Willow's abdomen, not-at-all subtly demanding she give him a greeting.

Surprised, Willow said, "Oh, my!" But she complied with his request and reached down to awkwardly pat the dog's head.

"That's Buddy." Carol informed her before shifting gears. "I'll take you back to see the puppies."

Willow followed the other woman out to a utility room where several roly-poly puppies were playing and napping. Even though she had never been a dog person, Willow couldn't help but chuckle at the tiny blonde puffballs. They were so adorably cute, the sight made her chest hurt.

Looking around the clean, blocked-off room, Willow realized that these pups were obviously very well cared for. They looked healthy and happy, which set her mind at ease. She had heard horror stories of puppy mills that frightened her.

Stepping over the gate, Willow squatted down to get a closer look. The puppies took that as an open invitation to attack. They jumped at her and tried to climb up into her lap. Willow smiled happily as they vied for her attention.

She played with them for a long moment wondering how on earth she was going to pick which one she wanted. When her knees started to tire from squatting down, she stood and turned towards Carol.

"They're adorable, and they all look healthy and happy." Willow smiled at the other woman.

"Oh, yes." Carol said earnestly. "They are my little sunshines."

Smiling down at the rambunctious pups, Willow said, "I can see why. How can you stand to let them go to new homes? Don't you get attached?"

"I can't keep them all." Carol smiled at her before adding, "Besides, they go on to do great things."

Intrigued, Willow raised her brows. "Oh?"

The woman's initial nervousness at meeting Willow evaporated as she gushed about her talented puppies. "My goldens are specially bred to be well-suited for vital jobs like seeing-eye dogs, rescue dogs, and emotional companions."

Willow enjoyed how Carol's eyes lit up when she bragged about her dogs. "That's impressive," she told the woman honestly before asking, "Is there one in this litter that seems to be suited for television?"

"Hmm. I don't know…" Carol hedged.

"They're all gorgeous," she praised the adorable animals. Tilting her head to the side, she asked, "How did you know Star would work so well on Dash's show? Did she have certain characteristics that stood out?"

"Oh, I didn't know that was going to be her fate," Carol revealed. "When I met Grace and her daughter, Clover, I thought Star was just going to be a family pet."

Leaning in and smiling at the memory, Carol added, "I don't normally allow my pups to go to people who aren't going to challenge their minds by training them to work, but I had a good feeling about those two."

"Guess you were right about them," Willow smiled at the breeder. "But Star seems like she was born to be on television."

"Doesn't she?" The other woman shook her head, grinning from ear to ear.

It didn't seem like she expected an answer to her question, but Willow nodded anyway before asking, "Which of these puppies reminds you the most of Star's temperament?"

"Oh, I don't know. They all have their own unique traits and individual personalities," the other woman hedged again.

"But are any of them similar to Star?" Willow pushed her, starting to become frustrated and wondering how she would ever pick the right dog.

Before Carol could answer, Buddy chose that moment to rest his head over the gate, peering up at Willow with gorgeous milk-chocolate eyes.

7

*B*uddy gave Willow a soulful gaze, making her smile. "What's this guy's story?" Willow asked the breeder as she reached over to ruffle the lanky dog's fluffy ears.

Carol smiled down at the ruddy dog. "Buddy is my sweet boy." Scratching his lower back, near his tail, she adjusted her voice and pooched out her lips as she addressed the dog directly, "Aren't you, Mr. Handsome?"

The dog slowly wagged his tail in response to the attention. When Willow stopped rubbing his ears, he nudged her, insisting that she resume. Willow was utterly charmed by the sweet dog.

Turning to Carol, she said, "I can see why you chose to keep him for yourself. He's delightful."

"He is." Carol agreed, nodding. She paused for a moment before adding, "But I didn't exactly *choose* to keep him. He wasn't up to my standards to sell."

Willow felt her hackles begin to rise. How

could this loving, gorgeous dog not be up to standard? She raised a brow in Carol's direction. "He seems pretty great to me."

"Oh, he is wonderful," Carol clarified before going on. "In fact, he tested off the charts on his emotional IQ. He is one of the sweetest, most loving dogs I have ever seen. Goldens are known for being kind, but he is one in a million as far as that goes."

The woman smiled proudly down at Buddy. Willow felt frustrated by the woman's response. It sounded to her like Buddy should have been the pick of the litter. When Carol took too long to respond, Willow prompted her, "But…"

The verbal nudge prompted Carol out of her reverie. "But he didn't test well on the aptitudes needed to work in any of the vocations my dogs are normally trained for. He is a great pet, who can remember a few simple commands, but his mental acuity level means he will never be a highly-trained service animal."

Lifting her hand to whisper at Willow as if her words might hurt the animal's feelings, Carol said, "He's all heart, but light on brains."

Willow stooped down to cover the dog's soft ears with her hands. She couldn't believe the breeder was speaking about him like that right in front of him. Even if he couldn't understand every word, he had to at least get the sentiment, right?

Willow wasn't at all sure how much dogs understood. Since they could learn and obey commands, she had to assume they comprehended at least some human language.

Speaking directly to the animal, she said,

"Don't you listen to her, Buddy. You are hand-some, sweet, AND smart."

Buddy nuzzled into her neck as if he under-stood every word of her sentiment. His soft fur and sniffling nose made Willow giggle, like a young girl, at the attention.

"He seems to have taken a liking to you." Carol weighed in.

Willow smiled up at her, "Yeah, too bad he's your pet because he is an absolute sweetheart."

Tilting her head to the side, Carol assessed them before saying, "He just sort of became my pet by default. I didn't intend to keep him because he doesn't have the right genes to be bred. In fact, I already had him fixed."

Willow didn't appreciate the other woman's insinuation that Buddy wasn't worthy of fathering pups. Logically, she understood that there were too many dogs that needed homes to recklessly breed puppies, but she felt oddly protective of this dog and didn't like hearing something about him that could easily be construed as an insult.

Feeling defensive, she asked, "If he's not up to your standards, why did you keep him?"

Not seeming to sense the accusation in her tone, Carol said, "I kept hoping that he would catch up with his siblings, but he just never did. By the time I realized he wasn't mentally astute enough to be a working dog, he was too old to sell as a pet."

At Willow's horrified look, Carol clarified. "Families looking for a golden pup want to enjoy them as cute little furballs, not to get them as lanky teenagers. He stayed with me and has grown into a handsome, loving dog, but no one seems to want that."

If there was one thing Willow understood, it was being considered too old to be useful. She hated the idea of this kind soul being brushed aside for cuter, younger options. The empty heartbroken feeling of being past your prime is something she was sure translated between humans and canines.

Not understanding why anyone would choose an ornery, untrained puppy over a well-behaved dog, she said, "Isn't he already housebroken?"

"Yes, he's a champ about that," Carol confirmed, beaming. "He rings a bell on the door when he needs to go outside."

That had been one of the main things Willow had been worried about with getting a puppy. The idea of having her expensive Persian rugs soiled by puppy 'accidents' was not something she had been looking forward to.

Growing more confused by the minute, Willow asked, "And he's already through the mischievous chewing stage?"

"Yes, he's through all of that," Carol confirmed before shifting back to the topic at hand. "Does one of the puppies catch your eye?"

Willow turned to look at the room of squirming, rambunctious puppies. Only one was managing to sleep through its siblings' activity, but she felt sure it would get up and join their playtime soon. There was no denying the little buggers were adorable, but none of them had the soulful eyes of the dog standing by her side, leaning into her and practically begging for her to notice him, rather than the babies.

When realization dawned on her, she looked back at Buddy. His tail flapped a few times as if he could sense the direction her mind was going. Whispering near his ear, she said, "You're not too old at all, are you?"

Standing to face Carol, Willow said, "I'd like to adopt Buddy, if that's okay."

Carol quickly hid the flash of surprise that registered on her face. She obviously hadn't thought anyone would actually be interested in the mature dog. After she had a moment to think about it, she slowly nodded her agreement. She looked from the russet dog to the woman standing before her and back at Buddy before a wide smile spread across her face. "I think that's a magnificent idea."

Willow beamed as Buddy's tail whacked loudly between the wall and Willow's leg. Carol might not think his aptitude was up to par, but there was no denying that he knew exactly what was happening. The best part was, he was obviously thrilled to be going home with Willow!

8

*W*illow and Carol quickly settled the details surrounding Buddy's adoption. Even though Carol had offered to decrease the normal fee, since Buddy was older, Willow insisted on paying the full amount. She didn't want Buddy to feel like he was in any way inferior or unworthy, due to his age.

As the happy dog loped behind Willow to the front door, somehow seeming to know that he was supposed to go with her now, she decided that he was worth at least double the amount she had paid. A thrill raced down her spine at the realization that she had a new best friend.

Carol handed Willow a nylon leash, which she attached to Buddy's collar before opening the front door. Willow was delighted to discover that Buddy didn't even need the tether to her. He walked quietly right by her side without seeming inclined in the slightest to run away. He was perfectly content to stay near Willow--evidently knowing his place was now with her.

When they reached the car, Nico opened the back door for them. Buddy jumped in as if he knew exactly what he was supposed to do.

As the car pulled away, Willow looked back and saw Carol wipe a stray tear from her cheek.

For his part, Buddy never even glanced back at the home he had known up until this point in his life. He was Willow's dog now. The realization made Willow's heart thump with an odd mixture of thrilled delight and anxiety. This dog trusted her with his life. She vowed to make sure she was worthy of his unwavering faith in her.

During their car ride, Buddy sprawled out taking up most of the back seat, but he rested his head in Willow's lap. She absently stroked the soft fur on his head, ears, and chest. When he rolled over to put all four feet in the air, giving her a not-at-all subtle hint to rub his belly, she couldn't help but laugh at the silly dog.

Gravity made his gooey black lips flap back, revealing a plethora of gleaming white teeth. The result made it look like Buddy was beaming a happy smile up at her.

Unable to resist his charm, Willow complied by running her hands through the soft white fur on his belly. The dog sighed with contentment and savored the undivided attention from her.

"Ma'am?" Nico asked her rather sheepishly.

The driver normally didn't speak to her, unless she initiated the conversation. Since Willow wasn't big on small talk, they generally spent most of their rides in silence. It dawned on Willow in that moment that she was the one who caused most of her intimacy issues. Nico had been her driver for years. They should have moved beyond polite niceties. She was ashamed to admit––even to herself––that she didn't know anything about the man's personal life.

"Yes, Nico?" She tried to insert an extra layer of friendliness into her smile. If the man was reaching out to her, she wanted to be open to taking their professional relationship into a deeper level of companionship.

Dashing those hopes, Nico asked nervously, "Shouldn't we stop by the pet supply store before heading back to your house?"

Nico had never before questioned her directions regarding where he should drive her. She could tell by his concerned expression in the rearview mirror that he was already regretting doubting her directive.

Giving him a warm smile to reassure him, Willow said, "Of course, Nico. You're right."

The relieved look that washed over Nico's face was undeniable. Deciding to share some of her vulnerability with him, she admitted, "Buddy is my first dog… ever. It's a thrilling prospect, but also a bit overwhelming."

Evidently not ready to start even a tentative friendship with her, Nico gave her a curt nod before saying, "Yes, ma'am."

Sighing and realizing that she wouldn't be able to forge the bonds of friendship with anyone in an instant, she gazed out the window. Distracted by her thoughts, she evidently stopped rubbing Buddy's belly because he used one of his big paws to gently bat at her and remind her of her job.

Chuckling to herself, she resumed scratching his tummy and silently amended her previous thought. She might not be able to forge the bonds of friendship with any *people* in an instant, but this hairy, lovable beast was already gazing up at her as if her friendship meant the world to him. It was a heady, marvelous feeling. She just hoped she could live up to his resolute belief in her.

When they pulled into the parking lot for the pet superstore, Willow felt overwhelmed. She wasn't at all sure what all a dog needed and this store looked massive.

Trying once more to reach out to Nico, she said, "I'm not sure what all Buddy needs. Any chance you would be willing to come in with me?"

"I need to stay with the car, ma'am." Nico said in a no-nonsense tone, proving that he wasn't in any way open to her attempted outreach.

"Okay," she mumbled as he got out of the car to open her door.

The trip around the car evidently gave Nico time to realize how harsh he had been with her because once he had her door open, he leaned down to give her some sage advice. "The employees inside will be able to help you, but be sure to let Buddy pick a few of his own toys."

Willow's eyes lit up. "He can go in with me?"

"Of course," Nico smiled down at her, obviously amused that she didn't know more about having a pet.

Thrilled to be able to face this unfamiliar challenge with her new friend by her side, Willow stepped out of the car with a new sense of excitement.

Buddy stared up at her anxiously, politely waiting to see if he was invited to exit the vehicle.

"Come on, Buddy!" Willow said to the dog, making him jump excitedly from the car.

Glancing down at her black pants, Willow quickly realized they were covered in light colored fur. She swiped furiously at them, but the coating of Buddy's hair only seemed to move around and expand. Finally giving it up as a lost cause, she turned to look down at the sweet dog. "Guess I better get used to it, and stop wearing so much black, huh, boy?"

When Buddy blinked up at her as if he was desperately trying to understand her words, she ruffled his ears playfully and said in an excited tone that she knew he would understand, "Let's go in!"

The happy duo entered the previously daunting-looking store side-by-side. Willow couldn't help but wonder if everything would be made better by having Buddy by her side. She had a strong suspicion that he would improve every facet of her life.

As soon as they entered the massive store that had an odd sawdust odor, a college-aged girl in a bright blue vest approached them. Her nametag proclaimed her name to be "Kaley."

Kaley's steps faltered when she met Willow's eyes. It was obvious that she recognized the talk show host. Willow normally wore glasses and a wig as a disguise when she went out.

Wanting to put the young lady at ease, Willow

smiled warmly and said, "Hi, Kaley. I'm hoping you can help us."

"Of course, Ms. Winks." Kaley's pretty blue eyes were alight with excitement over the celebrity encounter.

"You can call me Willow." She said warmly before turning to look down at her new dog. "And this handsome fellow is Buddy."

Kaley proved that she had chosen the right profession by stooping down to talk to and pet Buddy. "Aren't you a sweet boy?" She asked the dog. He responded by flapping his tail happily.

Willow grinned down at them, already pleased by the interaction. It was obvious that Kaley loved animals, and based on Buddy's reaction, the feeling was mutual.

Getting to the matter at hand, Willow revealed, "I just got him tonight, and I don't have any dog supplies."

Standing, Kaley said confidently to Willow, "You've come to the right place. I'll help you get all set up."

Willow followed the girl, loading a red cart with everything the young lady suggested. By the time they went to the checkout, they had large-breed formulated kibble, big plastic food and water bowls, a royal blue collar, engraved metal tags from a machine, bone-shaped treats, a soft dog bed, and every toy that Buddy pointed out with his snout.

Leaving the store, Buddy pranced with his head held high as if he had just won the doggy lottery, but Willow knew the truth was that she was the lucky one.

$\mathcal{B}$y the time Nico dropped Willow and Buddy off at home and carried in their many purchases from the pet supply store, it was starting to get late. Willow let Buddy outside in her fenced-in backyard. He ran around sniffing and exploring before doing his business and returning to the door to be let back inside.

Smiling, Willow realized how grateful she was that he already had this skill down to a fine science. As he bounded inside and went to sit quietly in front of the bags on the counter that held the treats, she chuckled at the brilliant dog.

"How could that silly lady think you aren't smart?" Willow asked him out loud as she ruffled through the bags to get him the requested treat.

As he gazed up at her like she was a giant T-bone steak, Willow marveled at her good fortune in finding a dog that was already trained and so well-behaved. Ruffling his soft ears, she said, "I can't imagine anyone choosing one of those bratty puppies over you. I guess you were just meant to be ready when I needed you, huh?"

It dawned on her that she was already talking to the dog like he could understand every word. When he blinked up at her, it was all the answer she needed to her question. She and this dog were meant to be together. There wasn't any doubt about it.

When she said, "I'm beat. Let's go to bed," the dog followed her to her bedroom unquestioningly, already seamlessly assimilating to her routine. While they padded into her bedroom, Willow thought about how nice it was to have a companion who didn't complain about how early she liked to go to bed to get her beauty rest.

In her room, she pointed to the cushy dog bed she had placed on the floor next to her luxurious California king-sized bed. She had sprung for the most expensive dog bed the store had, of course. Nothing was too good for her new friend.

Buddy gave the dog bed a side-eyed look before walking over to try it out. With a great huff, he plopped down on it, curling himself into a surprisingly small circle.

"Good boy!" Willow praised him before heading into her en suite bathroom to change and get ready for bed.

Once her extensive nighttime routine of lightly dabbing eye creams and wrinkle preventatives onto her face, décolletage, and hands, she emerged from the bathroom. She almost tripped when she saw the dog sprawled out to what appeared to be three times his normal size, right in the middle of her bed.

"Oh, no." She told him firmly, which earned her a look that could only be described as sad puppy-dog eyes. The pathetic look warmed her heart, but she remained frozen in mid-step as she wondered what to do.

Buddy blinked up at her, silently pleading with her to give in. She didn't have the heart to refuse him. Making a snap decision as she crossed the room and climbed into the bed beside him, she said. "Okay, but just for tonight, since you're probably scared by being in a new home."

The dog flapped his tail happily against the bed covers. Despite her protestation, both of them knew that he wouldn't ever make use of the dog bed on the floor.

With a stuttered, contented sigh, he leaned his back into Willow's spine and promptly fell asleep. It only took about thirty seconds for Willow to realize her dog was a loud snorer.

Normally, snoring drove Willow batty, but she found Buddy's deep, loud breathing to be oddly calming. It was reassuring to know that he was right there by her side. Before long, the emanating heat from his warm back lulled her to sleep.

Willow awoke just before her alarm went off feeling more refreshed than she had in months, despite the dread she felt about going into the studio today. She was sure that news of her demotion had spread like wildfire, and she wasn't looking forward to answering questions about it, or worse, being the recipient of pity-filled looks.

Watching from the kitchen window as Buddy

sniffed around her large backyard, she sipped her morning brew and decided she needed to make a plan of action. She had been so stunned by yesterday's announcement, she hadn't even asked how much longer she had with her current morning show. If history could be a guide, the studio execs didn't wait long to make changes, once they made up their minds.

She would need to devise a communication plan to say a proper goodbye to her fans from the talk show, and encourage them to watch her new game show. She needed to put a positive spin on it, so viewers didn't pick up on the fact that she was being demoted. If word of that got out, the new show would be doomed before it even really started. No one wanted to spend valuable time getting vested in a sinking ship.

This would be a tough day at work, but she would be a professional and hold her head up high. Having her new best friend, who already seemed to love her unconditionally, would make it easier to face the rumor mill.

Buddy could sit on the outskirts of the stage while her show aired, then she would take him upstairs and insist on a meeting with the studio execs to present her plan to have Buddy on her new show. The suits were already well-aware of the ratings boon a lovable dog could bring-- thanks to their marvelous experience with Star-- so she didn't think it would be too hard to convince them that Buddy would help make her game show a hit.

Deciding to focus on the positive, she took a deep centering breath. Despite her new friend and renewed hope for the future, her stomach churned nervously. Refusing to acknowledge the anxiety, she called Buddy inside, snuggled her head against his for a long moment, and went upstairs to get ready to face her challenging day ahead.

10

*A*s soon as Willow and Buddy entered the studio, Evelyn rushed up to them. "You're wanted upstairs… now."

The production assistant was normally a bit on the high-strung side, but her urgent tone took that to a whole new level.

Willow furrowed her brows together as she wondered what the big wigs could possibly want from her this time. They had just dropped their bombshell on her yesterday, so it couldn't be more bad news already… could it?

As she pondered this, Evelyn tapped her foot impatiently. Evidently, she wasn't willing to give Willow any time to mentally prepare for this meeting because she huffed out a frustrated breath and said, "Right now."

"Okay." Willow held up her hands in mock surrender before heading over to the elevator to ride up to the top floor. She punched the button angrily, not appreciating the unceremonious summons, since she normally used her extra time in the dressing room to mentally prepare for her live show. This meeting would throw off her whole schedule and leave her rushing through hair and makeup. She just hoped they didn't say anything to upset her further because she wouldn't have time to calm down before the show aired.

When the elevator arrived, she went to step on, but Buddy refused to budge. He looked warily at the elevator. "It's okay," she reassured him. "Come on, Buddy."

The dog looked at her as if she had lost her mind. She gently tugged on his leash, but he kept all four of his paws firmly planted on the mat that covered the slick marble tiles.

"Let's go." She tried one more time to get the dog on the elevator, but he was having no part of it.

Several people were waiting behind them to board the elevator. A man in a tailored suit said, "Excuse me," as he made his way around them. Others quickly followed his lead and the nearly-full elevator rose without Willow and Buddy.

The dog sat down and looked up at her with pleading eyes. She didn't want to make the kind-hearted animal do anything he was afraid of, but she needed to get upstairs.

She briefly considered leaving him with Evelyn or another P.A., but she knew they were all busy with their own jobs, and she didn't want to impose. Besides, after what happened with Star in this very building, she didn't trust anyone else with her faithful companion.

Not seeing another viable option, she turned towards the door that led to the stairs. It had been a long time since she had climbed more than a flight or two of stairs, but Buddy was worth it. Besides, it would be great exercise. Sealing her resolve, she looked down at the dog and said, "Okay, let's do this."

By the time they reached the fourth floor, Willow was panting and out-of-breath. For his part, Buddy didn't appear to be affected by the climb at all as he gazed up at her.

Pausing on the landing between floors to try to catch her breath, Willow brushed her hair back off her face. The last thing she needed was to be a sweaty mess when she met with the studio execs, but it looked like that was exactly what was about to happen.

After climbing another flight, she paused to put her hands on her knees. She never would have guessed that she was this out of shape.

Feeling a cool drip of sweat meandering down her side, she couldn't imagine how awful she must look. She prayed that she wouldn't see any of her fans before the show's stylists could get her fixed up.

Finally making it to the top floor, the duo emerged from the stairwell. The perfectly-coiffed receptionist, Amber, gawked at them before asking, "Are you okay? Is the elevator broken?"

"I'm fine," Willow panted before smiling and adding, "Or I will be once I catch my breath."

Amber didn't smile back. In fact, she looked like she was wondering if she should call emergency services. The elevator chose that moment to ding and a few people emerged from it.

When Amber turned her questioning gaze at her, Willow lifted her shoulders and explained, "Buddy wanted to take the stairs."

The other woman looked at her like she might have completely lost her mind. Shaking her head, she said, "They're all waiting for you in Conference Room 1."

That didn't sound promising at all. Conference Room 1 was the biggest in the entire office, and the fact that Amber had indicated 'they're all' waiting, meant this wasn't just a quick check-in with a vice president or two.

Nodding, Willow plastered a fake smile on her face as she and Buddy walked past the woman's desk towards the meeting. All eyes turned to look at the duo as soon as they entered the meeting room.

"Willow, thanks for joining us." The CEO said in an overly-friendly tone.

It was tempting for Willow to ask what other choice she had, but she managed to refrain. Instead, she nodded and smiled politely.

Looking down at the dog, her boss asked, "And who is this handsome fellow?"

"This is Buddy. He is going to be my on-air companion on the game show." All eyes were on her, so she felt the need to really sell the idea to them. "We all know what a blessing Star has been on Dash's show, so Buddy is bound to do the same for my new show."

She gave the man at the head of the table a genuine smile, hoping that her positive, resilient attitude about the unpleasant change would shine through as a glowing example of someone who deserved to keep her job at the studio.

"That's a great idea!" Her boss weighed in with obvious approval.

For the first time since learning of this impromptu meeting, Willow breathed a sigh of relief. That tentative relaxation was premature, though. She immediately tensed again when her boss said, "We'll get to test out that theory when your new show starts on Monday."

"Monday?" Willow asked, feeling perplexed about how she would be able to juggle two shows. She had been hoping for more time to come up with ideas to make her new show unique and fun.

Wanting to be a team player, but uncertain about facing the emotions of saying goodbye to her old show, while simultaneously showing excitement for her new one, she asked, "How long will the overlap be with both shows airing?"

"There won't be any overlap." The CEO beamed at her as if he was granting her a great favor.

"None?" Willow felt like her mind was not firing on all cylinders as she worked through what he meant. "But if the new show starts Monday, that means today is the last day of my talk show."

"Yep!" Her boss nodded as if she should be thrilled by this news.

"But I haven't prepared my goodbye speech to the audience. I was hoping to have a special show with highlights from past years and a star-studded finale." Willow frowned as she turned to look at the other faces in the room, seeking some support.

She didn't find any in the hard stares from around the huge table.

Raising his shoulders as if it was out of his control, even though they both knew it wasn't, her boss said, "Better hurry if you want to try to make any of that happen." Making a show of looking at his fancy watch, he added, "Just over an hour until your final show airs."

Buddy rested his head quietly on Willow's leg, offering his unquestioning emotional support. Willow absently rubbed his head. It was tempting to let this latest blow defeat her. Her instinct was to hunch her shoulders forward and wallow for a minute, but Buddy's kind eyes gave her a burst of energy.

Holding her head high, she shoved her chair back before standing to say, "Guess we better get busy then."

The tears would likely come later, but she forced herself to be strong in front of the suits. Turning to leave, she walked out of that meeting like a boss, with Buddy by her side.

*W*illow hastily scribbled her farewell speech on a scrap of paper, while she sat in the hair and makeup chair. Buddy had jumped into the chair next to hers and a stylist was brushing his reddish hair until it gleamed.

Her final show went off without a hitch. It flew by in a fast blur, despite the fact that Willow was trying to savor every last moment of it. She held her head high as she announced the show's end and promised that her fans could still see her on her new show, which she had hastily named in the dressing room, *Matched*.

It was a simple name that clearly conveyed the show's intent. Even though she had been rushed, she felt confident in the choice. Besides, she had announced it on the air, so the studio's bigwigs would be hard pressed to force her to change it now. She wanted to make this new show her own, so if it sank or did incredibly well, she wouldn't have anyone to blame or thank but herself––and sweet Buddy.

A tear threatened to fall as she made her final farewell to her loyal fans, but she managed to keep it at bay. She wanted to put a positive spin on this change, and for the most part, it seemed to work.

The highlight of her final show was when she introduced Buddy to her viewers. The in-studio audience ooh'd and aah'd appropriately over the gorgeous dog. He sat there like a champion show-dog, absorbing their adoration. It was already obvious that he would easily adapt to show business.

He didn't flinch at the bright lights or when the crowd clapped loudly, even when some high-pitched whistles pierced the air after Willow's final farewell. He also stayed glued to her side while she remained on the set signing autographs and posing for photos with each fan that waited to see her.

She normally wasn't one to enjoy sharing the spotlight, but Willow found she wasn't envious at all when people asked for pictures with Buddy. She wanted the world to grow to love her sweet dog as much as she already did, and the best place to start was with her existing fan base.

For his part, Buddy ate up the attention from the strangers, but he remained glued to Willow's side. He looked up regularly to check in with her to make sure she approved of his behavior. Each time, she gave him a reassuring pat to let him know he was doing exactly what she wanted. The eager-to-please dog preened at her approval.

Once they had greeted everyone who waited

and the studio was cleared of fans, the duo walked up the single flight of stairs to Willow's dressing room. Someone had added a smaller star under Willow's name with 'Buddy' scrawled in fancy lettering, just like Star's name was displayed just under Dash's on that duo's dressing room.

Willow couldn't help but smile when she saw the addition to her door. Buddy had evidently already won over the crew and earned his spot at the studio. It had taken her years to earn their respect, but she didn't begrudge her sweet dog their acceptance. In fact, it would make her transition much easier if Buddy was beloved by all.

When they walked inside, she was delighted to see an enormous bouquet of yellow roses on her dressing table. The card was addressed to Willow and Buddy. It read, "Congrats on many years of success and best wishes on your new adventure. Break a paw! Dash and Star."

She smiled at their silly dog version of the classic theatre idiom suggesting performers 'break a leg,' rather than uttering the words 'good luck,' which was superstitiously believed to bring the opposite.

Staring at the card, Willow allowed her eyes to water. Dash had written the perfect words by acknowledging her now-former talk show, while being encouraging about her new challenge. It dawned on her then that even though Dash was the closest thing she had to a friend at work, he probably didn't write this kind note himself. This thoughtful gesture had his wife, Grace's, name written all over it.

Making a snap decision, Willow decided that

Grace was precisely the person she needed to see right now. The women were on friendly terms, but had never been what anyone would call friends. Willow blamed herself for that, since there wasn't a kinder person in the world than calm, sweet Grace.

Willow knew she needed to reach out and be a friend, if she wanted to have any friends, and Grace was the perfect person to start with. Besides, Buddy would love visiting the treats side of Grace's flourishing bakery.

After Nico parked in front of the quaint bakery and held the car's door open for them, Willow's stomach felt like it was filled with fluttering butterflies. It had been a long time since she had reached out to anyone hoping for friendship. She felt sure that Grace was too kind to shun her, but she didn't want to take advantage of the woman's sweet nature.

It was Buddy, who gave her the encouragement she needed as Nico stood there, patiently holding the car's door open for her. After the second nudge from her dog's snout, Willow chuckled and said, "Okay, boy. I'm going."

When she invited the dog to jump out of the car, he did so before happily loping along by her side. She hadn't ever before imagined how wonderful it would be to not have to go places alone. Even though he wasn't human, having Buddy by her side gave Willow a newfound confidence that she hadn't enjoyed for a long time... if ever.

Grace's bakery was hopping with patrons, but the busy woman still paused to give Willow a friendly smile and warm greeting. Not wanting to take advantage of her celebrity, Willow took a number and waited for her turn to be helped.

When a perky girl with a high, bouncy ponytail called her number, Willow felt a surge of disappointment, but she tried not to let it show on her face.

"I'll take care of Ms. Winks and Buddy," Grace told the girl, before adding, "If you'll finish getting these peanut butter bones packed for Mr. Wong and Luna?"

The girl nodded cheerily and set about finishing Grace's customer's order.

Coming around the counter and wiping her hands on her bright blue apron with smiling pink-frosted gingerbread cookies on it, Grace pulled Willow into a warm hug. Willow felt the urge to cry into the loving woman's shoulder, but she didn't want to seem crazy, since she didn't know her that well, so she managed to refrain.

"I'm so glad to see you." Grace said sincerely near her ear before bending down to greet Buddy. "Aren't you a handsome man?" She asked the dog, making his tail flap in answer.

Standing back up, Grace said to Willow, "He has a lovable face that is perfect for television, just like Star."

It dawned on Willow then the she hadn't yet uttered a word to Grace, yet this fantastic woman had already made her feel so much better. It was easy to see why Dash was so madly in love with her.

Not seeming to sense that Willow was silent, Grace circled back behind the counter and continued in her friendly fashion. "I only got to see bits and pieces of your show today because it's been crazy busy here, but it looked like you handled the entire ordeal like a champion."

"Thank you." Willow infused as much sincerity into her voice as she could, hoping the other woman would understand she appreciated so much more than just her kind words.

Grace seemed to have a knack for saying the right thing at precisely the right time. Thinking of that, Willow said, "Your husband sent me lovely flowers and a perfectly-worded card today."

"Did he?" Grace tried to act surprised, but Willow saw right through her act.

"Mm-hmm." Willow nodded to confirm before adding, "I'm guessing you were behind that wonderful gesture, so thank you."

Grace's cheeks turned a lovely shade of pink, confirming that Willow's guess was correct, but she said, "Of course." She brushed off the praise before giving her husband the credit. "I'll let Dash know you liked them."

Willow gave her a knowing nod, but didn't call her out further on covering for Dash. Smiling to herself, she wondered how reassuring it would be to know there was someone out there always looking out for her and truly being her teammate, like Grace and Dash obviously were to each other.

Buddy was already proving to be a wonderful companion, but as much as she liked to joke about it, he couldn't really fill-in as the special man in her life.

Envious of what Grace had found with Dash, but not begrudging them their happiness, Willow firmed her decision to try to forge a friendship with Grace. The other woman was exactly the sort of genuine, positive influence she needed in her life--much like Buddy.

"Any chance you can take a short break?" She asked Grace, feeling nervous about the other woman's answer.

"Sure!" Grace responded, already removing her apron and grabbing a couple of delicate flower-painted glazed cups to fill with hot tea. "It's a lovely day out. Let's sit outside," she suggested, and just like that... Willow had another new friend.

"Wait... so you mean to tell me that Darren Starr wears a wig, false teeth, and lifts in his shoes?" Grace bugged her eyes out at Willow over her teacup, obviously scandalized.

"Afraid so," Willow confirmed, nodding. "I had always considered the movie star to be a total heartthrob, so I thought I'd stop by his dressing room to greet him before the show. Seeing him without his hair or teeth took care of the little crush I'd always had on him."

"I would think so!" Grace hooted with laughter at the idea of the vain superstar being flawed and human. Shaking her head once her giggles subsided, Grace said, "I guess even celebrities are human, just like the rest of us."

"Absolutely," Willow agreed, having seen her fair share of the unflattering side of flawed celebrities.

Nodding, Grace said, "I guess it must be hard

being put up on a pedestal all the time." Taking Willow's hand within her own on the two-top table, she added, "Being famous makes you seem somehow larger than life. It's easy to forget that you're human with real thoughts and feelings."

Although Willow was only locally famous, she still dealt with people having preconceived notions about how she should look, dress, and behave. It was comforting to have someone to talk to, who really seemed to understand the challenges of being recognized.

Proving that she was truly intuitive, Grace said, "Dash once had his picture snapped and posted online when he was taking the garbage out in his robe. It's like your right to privacy isn't the same as everyone else's."

"Yes," Willow nodded, so thankful that Grace got it. Most people rolled their eyes, as if her problems weren't real, if she tried to share some of the challenges of being a wealthy celebrity. She knew she was very fortunate and that she had chosen this path, but that didn't make the downsides any less frustrating.

"I won't step a foot outside anymore without my makeup done because there's always someone there to take a picture and post it online. The brutal comments when that happens are enough to send someone with a fragile ego like mine into a severe state of depression."

"Don't read those," Grace suggested.

Smiling, Willow nodded. "I've learned not to look at anything on the internet until it has been filtered by one of the studio's assistants."

"Good idea," Grace weighed in before revealing, "Dash used to read through all of that, but people can be so mean and hurtful. I don't think he even bothers to look at it anymore."

"That's because he's happy and madly in love. He doesn't worry what anyone else thinks." Willow guessed and was fairly confident she was right.

Grace's pretty blush confirmed that she knew her unconditional love for Dash was what made him confident enough to live his life without fearing public opinion. In turn, that happy assurance was precisely what made Dash almost universally beloved. Willow wished she could find a relationship that would set her own constant worries at ease.

Proving how intuitive she was, Grace changed the subject. "So, you're going to be setting everyone else up on dates on this new game show. What are we going to do about *your* love life?"

Willow liked it that Grace had said 'we' as if she had a vested interest in Willow's happiness. Perhaps they were already forging the bonds of true friendship. Since Grace seemed to be awaiting an answer, Willow tilted her head to the side and said, "What love life?"

Grace set about suggesting mutual acquaintances for Willow to date. When she suggested Miles, the greasy, smarmy executive producer of Dash's show, Willow said firmly, "Ewwww... no."

The options of available, straight men of a certain age were severely limited--as Grace quickly discovered. Willow had already been acutely aware of the problem.

"We could try an online dating site." Grace suggested once she ran out of viable options.

"I don't think so." Willow shook her head to shoot down that idea. Smiling down at her dog, who was sitting patiently by her chair, she leaned down to pat his head and said, "Maybe Buddy is meant to be my main squeeze."

Chuckling, Grace said, "Buddy is great, but we need to find you a human male that makes your heart leap when he enters the room."

Willow liked the sound of that, but doubted that it was in the cards for her. Rolling her eyes, she quipped, "Good luck finding him. I've been trying for, ahem-ahem," she fake-coughed into her hand, "years and haven't had any luck."

The women shared a laugh over that. Sensing that Grace probably needed to get back to work, Willow reluctantly stood to leave. She grabbed the slip of paper on which Grace had written down the name of her preferred vet, Dr. Keller, and the location of their favorite dog park by the ocean.

After giving Grace a warm hug, Willow took Buddy to the car. She couldn't help but smile as she realized she already had a second new friend. At this rate, she would be living a fulfilled, happy life in no time. Lifting her chin and grinning, she decided that perhaps she didn't need a man after all.

illow racked her brain all weekend for a way to make her new game show unique and fresh. Matchmaking gimmicks abounded, so she needed a way to make her show stand out. She wanted her viewers to be clamoring to see what was going to happen on the next episode.

If she didn't find a way to make her show so riveting that people couldn't stand to miss an episode, her ratings would be doomed before she even started. After all, she was competing with well-known, long-running nationwide game shows. She needed to give viewers a reason to tune into her, rather than the competition.

She thought about sending couples on dream dates where the studio picked up the bill for an unforgettable, classy evening, but that felt tired and overdone. She considered putting two strangers together in a locked room and making them figure out how to work together to escape, but that felt contrived, and she had the feeling most couples would end up hating each other.

As each idea surfaced, she quickly shot it down. She just couldn't seem to come up with the perfect hook.

Looking down at her ever-present dog, she asked him, "What can we do to make this show a smashing success?"

He blinked up at her as if trying to tell her something. Smiling and ruffling his ears, she said, "You're going to be there, so I don't know how anyone could resist tuning in, but we need to figure out a way to make our matchmaking intriguing."

Her Sunday-night jitters were kicking into high gear, especially since tomorrow she would be tackling a completely new adventure. She walked into her closet to pick out an outfit to wear to the studio in the morning. Even though her stylists had her change for the show, she liked to look nice when she arrived, since fans were often milling around outside in hopes of catching a glimpse of one of their favorite local celebrities.

Deep down, she knew that most of them were actually waiting for Dash and Star, but maybe with the addition of Buddy, she would start to be a bigger draw. The vast majority of looky-loos were gracious and excited to see her, anyway. Only rarely, did someone point out that she wasn't the one they were here to see.

Deciding to wear a colorful silk scarf to dress up her planned outfit for tomorrow, she pulled out her two favorites. She held up one, then the other, to her deep purple shirt. Unable to decide between the two, she held one in each hand in front of Buddy. "Which one should I wear?" she asked the dog.

She had heard once that dogs were practically colorblind, so she felt a little silly asking his opinion on the topic, until he used his long snout to indicate the one in her right hand.

"Excellent choice," she beamed down at him before turning to hang the other scarf back in its spot.

As she put the scarf he had selected on the hanger with tomorrow's shirt, her eyes lit up with an idea. "That's it!"

The production staff from her previous show had been pared down, since this game show was only thirty-minutes, rather than sixty, and it was to be taped, instead of aired live. Willow hoped that the missing individuals had been reassigned to other duties at the studio, instead of fired.

Guilt over not being able to attain better ratings threatened to rise up in her throat as she looked at the empty chairs around the familiar room. Scratching Buddy's ears, she silently vowed to do better this time around.

Diverting her attention, her director, Michael, whom she had worked with for many years, gave her a perplexed look before asking, "So, you want the *dog* to be the matchmaker?"

"Yes!" she enthused, unable to hide her excitement over her idea, despite the incredulous tone of his question.

Michael searched the other eyes in the room. "Anyone else have any other ideas?"

His hopeful question was greeted with blank stares.

After a long pause, the director gave an exaggerated sigh before saying, "Okay, we need to start production today, and I'm not hearing any alternative suggestions, so I guess our careers are dependent on the whims of a dog. Let's hope he knows what he's doing."

Willow hated to put so much pressure on Buddy's shoulders, but the happy dog didn't seem to sense that the jobs of everyone in the room were dependent on him being a hit on the show. Instead, he wagged his tail excitedly, not seeming to have a care in the world.

rustrations were high all around the set as Buddy blinked up at Willow, not seeming to understand what she wanted him to do. Willow knew the eager-to-please dog would pick one of the three men for the bubbly contestant, if Willow could just make him understand what she wanted.

She had already introduced the female contestant, Mandy, and talked to the woman about what she wanted in a man. Now it was time for Buddy to select his choice among three men for the woman to go out with, but he had his butt firmly planted on the ground next to Willow and was showing no inclination to go anywhere near the men.

Michael huffed in annoyance. "I thought you said he was a natural at this."

"He is." Willow defended her idea to involve the dog in the show as the official matchmaker.

"Right." The director let sarcasm drip in his

tone before giving a gruff shout to the room at large. "Let's take five."

Once the break started, Buddy seemed to relax. He leaned on Willow's leg, silently requesting a scratch. She gladly complied with his demand. "We just need to figure out a way to communicate to you what we want you to do, don't we, boy?"

Willow didn't care that others could see her having a full conversation with her dog. If the tabloids were going to call her an eccentric celebrity, she might as well own it. Besides, Buddy was better company than most of the people she knew.

Grace walked up to the duo on the stage, greeting Willow with a warm smile and Buddy with a quick rub that made his tail flap. Willow hadn't realized her new friend was in the studio audience, but she was glad to see her. Slicing straight to the problem at hand, Grace assured her, "He'll get it."

"I hope so," Willow said, before admitting, "My entire career is riding on it."

Putting a comforting arm around Willow's shoulders, Grace offered, "Maybe Dash could help. He has trained Star to do loads of tricks."

"Thanks," Willow said, but her heart wasn't in it. She doubted the studio execs would give her that much time. If they didn't shoot a pilot episode of the show that wowed the audience, the show would quickly be cancelled and forgotten.

Shaking her head, Willow said, "Buddy helped me pick which scarf to wear with this morning's outfit, so I thought sure he would be able to choose between three eligible bachelors for our contestants."

"Hmm." Grace furrowed her brow, obviously working on an idea. "What if we had each of the bachelors hold a scarf. Maybe that would cue Buddy that he's supposed to choose one."

Liking Grace's idea, Willow began to feel fresh hope that this crazy show might actually work. "It's worth a shot," she told her friend, before flagging down an assistant and requesting her to track down and bring every scarf in the building to the set.

Before long, the harried assistant returned with several scarves and filming resumed. Willow displayed the selection of floral, striped, and solid colored scarves on her forearm.

Walking over to the first bachelor, she said to him, "Pick a scarf."

When he went to quickly grab one, she added mysteriously, "Choose wisely because the fate of your love life may depend on it."

He smiled, but still chose the plain royal blue one.

"Why did you select that one?" She felt truly intrigued and wondered if this might be a fun and unique way to get to know the male contestants.

"Blue is my favorite color." He said simply.

Plastering on a smile, Willow said, "Okay. You're a man of few words, I guess."

Moving on to the man in the second seat, she said, "Which one do you choose?"

This man gave it more thought. His hand hovered of the red, white, and blue striped scarf, but he ended up selecting the brightly colored floral one.

"Hmm. Tough choice, huh? Why did you end up selecting the flowers?"

Proving he was a smooth operator, bachelor two said, "I thought this was the one Mandy would like best. If chosen for the date with her, I will bring real flowers like this for her."

"Ohhh... Very nice." Willow weighed in on his charming answer, truly starting to enjoy herself for the first time since they had started filming.

Moving to the third man, she said, "Okay, bachelor number three, the pressure is on. Which scarf do you choose?"

The man perused the scarves, obviously taking the selection process very seriously. He rubbed the silk fabric of the brightly colored, happy looking polka dot one between his fingers, but put it down. Next, he glided his fingers over the black chiffon with gold embroidery.

Willow thought sure he was going to pick that one, so she was shocked when he quickly bypassed it and picked up the red, white, and blue striped one.

"Final answer?" she teased him, since he had seemed so indecisive.

"Yes." He now sounded sure of his choice.

"Why the stripes?" she asked before pointing the handheld mic at his mouth.

"It reminds me of Memorial Day and the Fourth of July," he revealed. "I am a patriot, and I love this country with all of my heart."

"All of your heart?" Willow nudged him playfully. "I hope you're leaving room in there for a special woman."

"Oh, yes, ma'am," the man answered politely before adding, "I can't wait to find someone to spend the rest of my life loving and cherishing." Coming from anyone else, it might have sounded like he was pandering to the camera, but this young man seemed sincere.

"Wow. Okay, then." Willow walked back to the other side of the divider that was separating the stage so Mandy couldn't see the contestants. Looking into her eyes, Willow said, "It would be tough to choose between them, but who would you choose?"

Mandy milked the moment as she thought over her options. "I can't decide between number two and number three."

The hype man evidently encouraged the in-studio audience to jump in with their opinions because they started yelling out numbers. Willow heard lots of 'twos' and 'threes,' plus a few, scattered 'ones.'

Mandy flashed a beaming white smile at them. Still sounding a little uncertain, she said, "Two?"

The audience clapped their approval of her choice. Willow surprised them when she said, "Let's see if Buddy agrees."

Leading the dog to the other side of the partition, she asked him, "Which scarf Buddy one, two, or three?"

The dog sat there blinking, obviously uncertain what she wanted from him. She walked closer to the contestants and lifted each man's arm holding the scarf as she said to her pet, "One, two, or three."

Buddy blinked up at her, motionless. Willow could feel her career spiraling down the toilet as she willed herself not to cry. There would be plenty of time for tears once she was unemployed––most likely tomorrow.

At a loss for how to communicate her wishes to the dog, she collected the scarves from the men. "It looks like we'll be going with Mandy's choice. Congratulations, bachelor two!"

Even though she had tried to insert an appropriate level of enthusiasm into her voice, she knew it fell painfully flat. Without Buddy selecting the bachelor, this show was too much like countless others. It would be lucky to make it past the pilot show.

Looking into camera two with the scarves draped across her arm, she started to give her closing remarks, promising to have more contestants next time, as well as a follow-up on how Mandy's date went.

Buddy turned to her as she was speaking and nudged the blue scarf with his nose. Willow almost couldn't believe her eyes.

With renewed excitement in her tone as she held up all three scarves for his inspection. "Is that the one you choose, Buddy? The blue one?"

Wagging his tail, obviously excited that she was so pleased, he nudged his head up into the blue scarf again.

Turning to the audience, she said, "Okay, Buddy has spoken. We'll send Mandy on a date with bachelor one to see if it's a love match."

Her eyes were alight with a fresh idea when she decided the studio could spring for a second date to amp up the dramatic suspense. "Then we'll send her on a date with the bachelor she chose. Which man will Mandy prefer--the one she selected or Buddy's choice? Tune in to *Matched* next time to find out."

Willow gave the camera her signature wink and signed off the show to raucous applause from the in-house audience.

15

From the in-studio audience's excited reaction, it was clear that this new show was going to be a hit. Willow beamed as they clapped and whistled for her and Buddy. The dog sat regally by her side, lapping up the attention and praise.

Even Michael, who had been completely skeptical about Buddy's role on the show, smacked her jovially on the back and said, "Great show." She knew from years of working with him that this was incredibly high praise.

Willow couldn't wait to see how Mandy's dates went, and based on how Willow's Reel Life social media feed blew up after the show aired, neither could anyone else. The show's hashtags were trending, and she felt relevant again for the first time in longer than she cared to admit.

Basking in the moment, she sat outside on her home's balcony to enjoy the gorgeous sunset over the water. Buddy snoozed happily by her side. It had been a long time since she had felt this relaxed and happy, and it was mostly thanks to her faithful new companion.

As she stared peacefully out over the water and watched the last bit of the sun sink past the horizon, she realized that--despite her demotion--she now had a renewed sense of vigor about her job. She honestly couldn't wait to see how Mandy's dates went with the two bachelors. There was no denying that she secretly hoped the woman liked Buddy's choice better than her own, but either way it was bound to make for an exciting show to see how things worked out for the contestants.

Rocking in her chair as she sipped her favorite Chardonnay from Dorma Valley Winery, she realized that she hadn't felt this jazzed about her talk show in a very long time. Maybe it had been time for a change, and this was beginning to feel like a good one.

Buddy rolled onto his side and began snoring with vigor. She smiled and realized there was no doubt about it... Even though she had initially balked about it, this change had been exactly what she needed.

When Nico opened the door for Willow and Buddy at the studio, the line of people waiting outside the building went wild. They clapped and cheered for them in a manner that Willow hadn't enjoyed in a very long time--if ever.

She beamed and waved at the crowd before promising to see them inside. Buddy pranced happily at her side as if he knew he was beloved by all.

As they walked up the single flight of stairs and through the maze of offices to their dressing room, Willow was delighted to see that her coworkers were making eye contact with her again. She hadn't realized how much their averted gazes had bothered her when she had been a failing talk show host. She much preferred the open friendliness and well-wishes she and Buddy received as they walked through the studio's hallways.

Before long the duo was announced to be camera-ready and they made their way down to the stage. Willow found that she enjoyed the flexibility of taping the show, rather than airing live. If they were a minute or two late, it didn't matter. If she made a mistake or said the wrong thing, they could do a re-take.

She hadn't realized how much stress she put on herself to be perfect when she was doing the live show, but now that the pressure had been relieved, she felt like a new woman.

Thanks to Willow's many years of practice, the show went off without a hitch. Just knowing that if she made a mistake, it could easily be fixed, helped her to keep things running smoothly.

Willow and the in-studio audience were delighted to hear that Mandy's date with the blue scarf man, Joe, whom Buddy had chosen, went better than the date with the man Mandy had chosen herself. Mandy admitted that she had initially been skeptical, but her eyes lit up as she spoke about the instant connection and chemistry that she'd enjoyed with Buddy's bachelor that she hadn't felt with the other man.

Mandy asked Joe if he would go on another date with her. He happily agreed before giving her a sweet kiss on the cheek. The two were declared as 'Buddy-Matched' with upbeat music and on-screen fanfare, and the studio audience went wild.

Buddy's nails clicked on the floor as he practically danced with happiness. He seemed to sense that he had done a good job.

During the break, Mandy and Joe left and the next contestants were shuffled onto the stage. In a surprise twist, Buddy and the new woman chose the same bachelor.

Sparks were already flying onstage when this new couple met, so Willow felt confident that they would be another great match. Buddy was proving himself to be quite the matchmaker, and in the process, he had almost single-handedly gotten Willow's career back on the right track.

As the weeks went by and Buddy successfully matched couple after couple, the famous duo quickly became the toast of the town. Willow felt like she was on top of the world, which made the chill-inducing, spine-tingling threat seem like an even further fall.

16

*C*aleb McCreery was a no-nonsense, low-frills kind of guy. Nothing made him happier than a night spent outside with friends by a bonfire, telling tall-tales, roasting hotdogs, and drinking a chilled beer from a bottle.

He kept in shape by baling hay and harvesting grapes for local farmers between bodyguard gigs. Flexing his muscles in front of a mirror at the gym was not his scene. He preferred, instead, to put in a long day of hard work, for an honest day's pay. Keeping his body lean, strong, and capable was an added perk of his solid work ethic.

After watching his single-mother work tirelessly, struggling for years to make ends meet to provide for him and his four sisters, Caleb had no sympathy for lazy, coddled celebrities, who had no idea what a *real* day of work entailed. That's one of the main reasons he had settled in Redwood Cove when he moved back to California's Gold Coast after his stint in D.C.

The job prospects abounded for a bodyguard further south, around Hollywood, but he didn't have the patience to deal with famous people, who felt like they were entitled merely because they could regurgitate words and actions that were scripted for them. He would rather deal with sporadic bouts of unemployment than risk his life for a person he didn't respect.

"Willow Winks?" He barked into his cell phone, feeling certain he'd heard the silly alliterative name before, but uncertain where.

As the fast-talking woman on the other end of the line spoke, he caught bits and pieces as he tried to place Willow's name. "Talk show… television… Buddy… matchmaking game show."

When his familiarity with the name clicked into place, he tried not to let the surge of disappointment overwhelm him. It had been a long time since he'd had a bodyguard gig, and the extra money would have been nice.

His mother's aging house needed a new roof. He'd already repaired it so many times that the patches now needed to be patched.

As much as he enjoyed working in the fields, the work was labor intensive, but light on pay. He wasn't a materialistic person. In fact, he was perfectly happy in his simple studio apartment as long as he got to spend his weekends outside camping, fishing, hiking, or entertaining his nieces and nephews.

There was no denying that the extra cash would be nice, though. If the gig lasted long enough, he could get his mother a replacement roof and have enough left over to get that new

Patagonia backpack he'd had his eye on for months.

Knowing that his patience would wear thin with a vain, pampered celebrity, he took a deep breath, kissed that big payday goodbye, and snapped into the phone, "I don't work for celebrities, Evelyn. Goodbye."

Just as he was getting ready to punch the red dot on the screen to disconnect the call, he heard the desperate woman plead, "Wait! Please."

Something in her frantic tone made him pause and hold the phone near his ear. He waited silently, confident that nothing she could say would change his mind.

"I've heard you're the best." She buttered him up. "And we can't have anyone but the best keeping Willow and Buddy safe."

"There's a man, too?" His curiosity was suddenly piqued.

"A male dog." The woman clarified before adding, "Buddy is an incredibly talented, super-famous golden retriever."

"That part doesn't sound bad at all," Caleb admitted before shaking his head adamantly. "But I can't deal with celebrities. They are too full of themselves and impossible to please. Most of them behave in a way that makes me *not* want to save them, but that is a contradiction to my job--which I take very seriously, by the way."

"I've heard that about you," Evelyn revealed. "And that's why we need you. Willow and Buddy are vital to our network. Their safety is of the utmost importance."

Beginning to feel bad, Caleb finally said, "Look,

I'm not going to take the job myself, but I can give you contact information for a few colleagues of mine that are excellent bodyguards."

"We don't want excellent. We want the best." Evelyn insisted.

Caleb was surprised by the woman's determination and persistence, but he wasn't willing to budge on this. If he hated his client, it might make him hesitate for a fraction of a second when it mattered most, and he couldn't abide by that.

Just as he was getting ready to tell her to forget it, Evelyn found his weak spot. "We'll triple your normal fee."

A vision of his hardworking mother's relieved face at the news that he had earned the money to replace her roof flashed into his mind. He wanted to see in real life the worry lines ease from her brow like they had in his mental image. Rolling his eyes up to the ceiling, and taking a deep breath, he said to Evelyn, "Now you have my attention."

17

*C*aleb held the threatening note up to the light. The tiny letters had been precisely cut from magazines in perfect squares that were then glued to the white, lined paper. The level of perfection of the straight cuts and lines made it obvious that this note had been made by someone who was either incredibly persnickety or had way too much time on their hands.

"Do the police think it's a copy-cat from the criminal who abducted Star?" he asked the room at large.

All eyes stared back at him, blinking blankly. Finally, the suit at the head of the table leaned forward and answered. "They aren't sure. The woman who committed that crime was captured and is facing punishment, but this note does feel eerily similar to the one the studio received just after Star's abduction."

"But no one has been taken this time, right?" Caleb wanted to make sure.

"Not yet," The executive revealed before folding his hands together in front of him. Giving Caleb an earnest look, he said, "We can't lose Willow or Buddy. Their ratings are soaring."

Caleb widened his eyes over the man's blatant admission that he was so worried about the stars merely because of their popularity with the viewers. Unable to keep the sarcasm completely at bay, Caleb said, "It's touching to see how much you care about them."

Missing his sarcastic tone, the man replied, "Oh yes, they are two of our biggest stars. Having one or both of them kidnapped would be a publicity nightmare."

Shaking his head over the crass viewpoint, Caleb said, "Well, now, we can't have that."

The executive's vehement "No" made it obvious that he honestly believed that he and Caleb were on the same page.

Deciding the obtuse man would never see what was wrong with looking at his employees as dollar signs, Caleb asked, "Does she know about the threat?"

Sitting back in his chair, the businessman said, "Not yet. We thought you should be here when we break the news to her."

"Great," Caleb muttered under his breath, realizing that the drama was just getting started.

Willow Winks was even prettier in person than on-screen. Of course, Caleb had never actually sat down and watched her talk show or her popular new game show, but he'd still managed to see her likeness on commercials, billboards, and even a city bus or two.

She had a handsome, healthy-looking dog with her. Caleb had always been a sucker for a woman who liked dogs, but he wasn't going to let his carefully erected walls down around this lady. She was the epitome of the word 'diva.' Caleb couldn't stand divas. His youngest sister, Cassidy, sometimes tried to act like one, but he wouldn't put up with any entitled behavior from her. She knew he had no patience for it.

The dog seemed to sense that Caleb was different from the others in the room. Since Caleb's chair was scooted back from the conference table, the animal walked right over and plopped his butt down practically on top of Caleb's boots.

"Well, hi there." He leaned down to scratch the happy dog.

"His name is Buddy," Willow told him.

Caleb liked it that she didn't assume he would know the dog's name just because they were on a television show. Even though he had already been aware of the famous canine's name, for some reason, Caleb pretended he was learning it for the first time. Nodding, he said, "Hey, Buddy! Aren't you a good boy?"

The dog's tail flapped excitedly at the use of his name and the undivided attention.

When Caleb looked up and caught Willow smiling down at them, he was startled to see how beautiful and vivid her blue eyes were. The camera didn't do them justice. Instead of saying that, he blurted out, "You don't look as old in person as you do on television."

He could tell by the way Willow's face scrunched up that it had been precisely the wrong thing to say upon meeting her. He had meant it as a compliment, but it didn't come out that way. He wanted to take it back and clarify that her eyes were mesmerizing and that she looked younger than he expected, but he sensed that he had already flubbed up this introduction beyond redemption.

"Umm. Thank you?" She finally said as she sat in the only available chair, next to him.

She then turned and bugged her eyes out in the direction of one of the only other women in the room filled with executives. The females shared a non-verbal conversation, and he could tell that he hadn't made a favorable impression on either of them.

Wanting to move the focus away from his awkward comment and steer the meeting back to the matter at hand, he slid the note across the glossy tabletop in Willow's direction.

Caleb could tell the moment it began to sink in with Willow what she was looking at. Her brows pinched together as she read the cobbled-together message.

I went on your show to get matched.
   And now my poor heart needs patched.
   The plan didn't work out at all.
   Your hosts are going to fall.
   Take the show off the air.

Or I'll accept that as my dare.
Kiss Willow and Buddy goodbye.
They better prepare to DIE.

Willow read the last line aloud, even though her voice sounded weak. When she repeated the line a second time, it came out as a question. "They better prepare to die?"

She looked up then and searched the faces of the others in the room. "Someone is threatening to kill us?" Her voice rose to a squeaky pitch at the end of her rhetorical question.

"I'm afraid so." The suit at the head of the table accepted his role as spokesperson for the rest of the group.

Willow's mouth opened and closed a few times as she processed this alarming news. As Caleb watched her, he realized that the threat was literally jaw-dropping, but he decided it would be wise to refrain from saying that.

When Willow finally found her words, they came out in a flurry of questions. "Have the police been notified? What are we doing to catch this wacko? Do we have any ideas about who it could be? Why would anyone want to hurt us? You aren't going to cancel the show, are you?"

Her questions were rapid-fired so quickly together, it wasn't possible for anyone to insert answers between them. When she finally paused, Caleb said to Willow, "Just take a moment to breathe. You've been given some shocking news, but now you're babbling."

He inwardly cringed at the condescending tone

of his own voice. Something about this lovely, frightened woman made him turn into a bumbling jerk.

"Babbling?... I'm Babbling?!?" Willow kicked her rolling chair back away from the table as she stood up.

When she turned her fiery gaze towards Caleb, he realized that he had gravely underestimated the shade of her blue eyes. They were nothing short of dazzling as they beamed a venom-filled storm of eye darts in his direction. The fury practically emanated off her in waves.

"Who is he? And what is he doing here?" She half-shouted to the room at large as she pointed at Caleb.

The head honcho used a placating tone with the temperamental star. "This is Caleb McCreery. He's your new bodyguard."

"Over my dead body," she seethed between gritted teeth.

Caleb rolled his eyes and said under his breath, "Oh great… Here we go."

"What did you just say?" she screeched.

Standing from his chair, Caleb stared down into those gorgeous eyes and said, "I said that I don't work with spoiled divas. Good day."

18

*W*hen Caleb made a move to ease past Willow to get to the conference room door, the booming voice of the studio's president filled the room. "Both of you sit down and shut up."

Caleb hadn't been treated like that since grade school, and he didn't appreciate it one bit. By the expression on Willow's face, it was obvious that she wasn't keen on being yelled at or ordered around, either.

The executive softened his tone. "Please have a seat. We are facing a very real and extremely frightening threat. Our nerves are all on edge, but we need to calmly discuss it like rational adults."

It was tempting for Caleb to storm out and tell them that this particular threat wasn't his problem, but the mental image of how happy his mom would be when he told her he was paying to have a new roof put on her house made him stay.

Reluctantly, he rolled his chair back to the table and took a seat.

Buddy tilted his head onto Caleb's leg. Unable to resist the sweet dog, he began absently rubbing the dog's soft fur on his ears.

Willow remained standing with her arms crossed, obviously still in a snit.

Her boss said, "Willow, please. Let's talk this through. We have to figure out a plan of action that we can all agree on. This isn't something we can simply ignore and hope it goes away."

Willow plopped back down into her seat, but she kept her arms crossed, still looking perturbed. Tossing her head in Caleb's direction, but refusing to make eye contact with him, she said, "He doesn't look big enough to be a bodyguard."

It was a stereotype Caleb was used to dealing with. Many people expected bodyguards to have big, hulking, and muscular body types, like the hired goons celebrities often traveled with-- mostly for show. In actuality, muscles weren't required in his line of work nearly as much as people believed. Quick reactions, the ability to read a room and find danger, and being willing to make the ultimate sacrifice, if needed, were the skills that made a truly outstanding bodyguard. Caleb knew he excelled in all three of these areas.

"I can take care of myself and anyone I'm being paid to protect." He said to the room, hoping to quell any further doubts about his physique. Although he was tall and strong, he was thinner than people expected him to be.

"Oh, we're supposed to just take his word on that?" Willow asked, obviously doubting his skills.

"No." Her boss answered matter-of-factly as he pulled a single sheet of paper out of a manila file folder. "I think we should look at his on-the-job record." Glancing at the paper, he said, "You were a uniformed division officer with the Secret Service for several years?"

Even though it was obvious the man already knew that to be the case, Caleb answered, "Yes, sir. I was on a protective mission with the U.S.S.S. at the White House."

Letting the air blow loudly out of her mouth, Willow said, "Were you the one who let the lunatic streak across the White House lawn?"

"No, ma'am." Caleb answered in a serious tone before adding, "That would not have happened on my watch."

He knew he sounded cocky, but he had every right to be. He was very good at his job, and he didn't appreciate having his finely-honed skills doubted.

Apparently unwilling to let up on him, Willow went on. "I thought the Secret Service was supposed to be a really exclusive position. Why were you let go?"

It raised his hackles that she assumed he had been fired, but he refused to let his annoyance show. Instead, he calmly turned to face her and said, "I decided to leave on my own. I was sick of D.C. traffic and dirty politicians." Opting to reveal a bit of his softer side, he added, "Besides, I missed my mama, and she lives just outside of Redwood Cove."

"Your mama?" Willow jumped on his admission. Turning to her boss, she acted like Caleb wasn't sitting right beside her when she asked, "You're going to put a *boy* who misses his mama in charge of our safety?"

Caleb didn't appreciate her tone or her reference to him as a boy. Just as he was considering storming out––for real this time––the studio boss slammed his fist on the gleaming mahogany table.

"That's enough!" He shouted, startling them all. "This danger is real." Pointing at Willow, he said, "Caleb is the best at what he does. You will let him do his job." Turning to Caleb, he said, "You will keep her and the dog safe."

With that, he got up and left the room. The others quickly followed his lead. Soon, it was just Caleb, Willow, and Buddy left alone in the room.

illow glared at the large abstract painting on the wall across from her. She could feel Caleb's presence beside her, but she refused to look in his direction. Besides, she had taken in his handsome, rugged appearance as soon as she entered the room––before the threatening letter bombshell had been dropped on her.

She knew that he was tall, lean, and young… too young. Still staring at the wall, she asked him, "What are you… 22 years old?"

"More like 27," he answered quickly before asking, "What are you… 45?"

Unable to keep from turning to glare at him, she snapped, "More like 37." She decided it was better to go with the lie she consistently told the press than to admit her real age. She didn't know this man at all, so she couldn't trust him not to leak anything he learned about her.

Ignoring her, he bent down to scratch Buddy's

shoulders and chest. The traitor dog leaned on the exasperating man as if he was the greatest person in the world.

Willow reluctantly admitted to herself that Caleb's obvious soft spot for dogs was somewhat endearing, as was his clear love for his mother. One lesson that had been ingrained in her brain growing up in Georgia was that you could tell a lot about a man's suitability as a potential love interest by the way he treated his mom.

Shaking her head, she wondered why she had even started to go down that path in her mind. Caleb most definitely was not a suitable love interest for her. He was annoying and young. Besides, she didn't want to distract him from his job. Her and Buddy's safety were evidently going to be dependent on him.

Deciding to take the high road and shift the conversation back to the task at hand, she lifted the letter before saying, "I guess we don't have to get along as long as you're willing to keep us safe."

"That I can do," he promised, giving her an unflinching stare.

Something about his confident tone and the way his chestnut brown eyes pierced into her, made her believe him. Trusting her gut, she said, "Okay, then. Let's do this."

"Yes, ma'am." Caleb used a no-nonsense tone, so it took her a moment to register his words when he thumbed a large, military green duffle bag on the floor behind them and said, "I brought my stuff, so I can move in now."

"Move in? With me?" Willow spluttered, not quite believing her ears.

Caleb gave her a look that clearly said he was wondering if she was daft before saying, "Yes, ma'am. I can't protect you and Buddy if I'm not with you."

"Well, I thought you would come with us when we are out in public and watch over things during the show." After pondering it for a moment, she added, "I have a state-of-the-art security system at my house. I should be safe there."

"Let's assume that the person who carefully pasted this letter together is truly crazy," Caleb started.

When he paused, Willow interjected, "I think that's a safe assumption."

Ignoring her snark, Caleb went on. "It sounds like he or she wants you and Buddy dead."

The flippant way Caleb referred to the threat made a chill race down Willow's spine, but she forced herself to remain calm and nod her agreement.

"So, we know the author of this letter is crazy and homicidal. As painstakingly as these cut-out letters have been placed on the paper, I'm going to go out on a limb here and say that this person is a meticulous planner. Do you think he or she would show up at your house without a way to get in as well as a weapon?"

When he looked expectantly at Willow she said, "No, but the alarm would go off..."

Before she could finish he said, "You're right. The alarm would go off, which would let you know that you and Buddy are in your house with an armed lunatic. At best, the police would be there in three to five minutes. Do you know how much can happen in three minutes? It's longer than you think." He pulled out his cell phone and set a timer.

They sat there in silence for what seemed to be an interminable length of time. When Caleb announced, "It's been twenty seconds," Willow almost couldn't believe that only that short amount of time had passed.

"Okay, I get the point. You can shut off the stupid timer." She grouched, before adding, "We don't want to be alone in the house that long with this person." Quickly brainstorming, she added, "Maybe I should have a panic room built."

"Maybe." Caleb seemed to be in agreement, until he said, "But what if you can't get to it in time, or what if the armed maniac is between you and the safe room?"

Willow shrugged her shoulders. Two panic rooms seemed excessive. She was starting to think that she might, in fact, need a bodyguard––at least until the police figured out who was behind this threat.

Not willing to give in that easily she asked, "But what if you're in the bathroom or asleep when the alarm goes off. No plan is foolproof."

"Nothing will happen to you while I am protecting you," he promised confidently.

Even though the logical side of her brain knew there was no way he could possibly know that, her gut instinct was to believe him. He seemed so sure of his abilities it was tough to continue doubting him.

After thinking it over for a long moment and

not devising any other options, Willow lifted her chin and said, "I trust you."

Returning her sincere gaze with one of his own, Caleb told her, "I'll do everything in my power to be worthy of that trust, ma'am."

20

*I*n a matter of weeks, Willow had gone from prattling around her big, fancy house alone to having two males in her space. There was no denying, the canine variety was much less disruptive and annoying than the human one.

Buddy seamlessly fit into her life. Caleb created chaos in his wake.

After their initial meeting where Caleb had seemed arrogant and rather rude, Willow had reluctantly decided to accept his presence in her life. Although it was a major inconvenience, it was better than the very-real possibility of facing an armed attacker alone.

Caleb's steadfast assurance that he would take care of her made her feel as safe as possible—considering she had a lunatic threatening her. Each week, like clockwork, a new letter arrived on Tuesday. They were consistently short, threatening, and filled with bad rhymes. They were also mailed from different public mailboxes around town each time, and they had no fingerprints or DNA from saliva on them, which gave the police very few clues to go on--other than the fact that it was likely a former contestant on the show. Whoever this nutcase was, he or she was incredibly careful and elusive.

As they re-read the fourth letter together, Caleb quipped, "I think we can rule out poets and other linguists as suspects."

Despite the dire nature of the warning note, Willow burst out with laughter. She immediately covered her mouth with her hand because it seemed wrong to be laughing about such a thing, but it felt good to forget for a moment about the ax dangling precariously over her head.

"I shouldn't be laughing about this." She looked up into Caleb's milk-chocolate brown eyes and noticed they were a very similar shade to Buddy's. The man didn't give her quite the same look of devoted adoration as the dog did, but Caleb's gaze had warmed considerably since their horrendous introduction.

"It's fine to laugh," he assured her. "Sometimes we all need some comedic relief--especially when we're under stress. You've been under an inordinate amount of stress for weeks, and you've been handling it like a champ."

Willow felt her cheeks heat at the compliment. It was high praise coming from him, since he never seemed to say anything kind to her. She was surprised to find that she liked having his approving gaze on her. It felt like stepping into the sunlight after a long bout of drizzling rain.

She shook her head and reminded herself that this was a purely professional relationship, forged out of necessity. Feeling uncomfortable with the warm look he was giving her, she looked away and busied herself with tapping her cell phone screen. Deciding to downplay her stoicism, she said, "It's not like I have any choice."

"I would have assumed you would be all drama, all the time."

And there they were... back to their normal state of him picking on her about being a pampered celebrity. She turned to glare at him and was surprised to find him giving her a wide, knowing grin. Secretly delighted to see that he had been teasing her, but pretending to be annoyed, she lightly smacked the back of her hand against his surprisingly firm chest.

It was the first time she had ever touched him. Even though it wasn't in any way an intimate touch, she was surprised by the jolt that tingled up her arm at the brief connection.

Considering the intense look Caleb gave her, she wondered if he had felt it too. She was almost certain that he had because he quickly averted his gaze and said, "Mickey will be coming soon to take over for the weekend."

"Great." She plastered on a smile, like she wasn't disappointed that it was time for their shift change already.

Mickey took his job seriously and never let his guard down, but he had absolutely no personali-ty––despite his fun-sounding name. During the weekends when he stayed near Willow's side, she honestly wondered if the stoic man ever smiled.

She couldn't even imagine him cutting loose and having fun.

Although Caleb slept in one of her guest rooms, making him on the job twenty-four hours a day, she still found herself wishing that he didn't need days off.

She couldn't even imagine how much the studio must be paying for her round-the-clock guards, but it didn't really matter, since the police didn't seem to be any closer to catching her stalker. They had interviewed each of the show's former contestants, but didn't have any evidence against any of them. They were expanding the search, since the first letter's hints that it was from a disgruntled contestant might have been a diversion.

Willow was curious about what Caleb did during his time away from her. The main question she wondered about was if he had a girlfriend, but she didn't feel like it was her place to ask about it.

Despite Mickey's focus on his job, he didn't instill the confidence in her that she was safe in the same manner that Caleb did. If they were ever going to have to face this maniac, she hoped that it would be during the week, when Caleb was on duty.

After Caleb filled Mickey in on the content of the latest letter and the lack of further activity for the week, he bent down to give Buddy a long goodbye scratch. "I'll see you Monday, sweet boy."

Willow was surprised at her annoyance over the fact that he obviously missed Buddy during his weekends away, but not her. It didn't make sense for her to feel that way, but that didn't negate the fact that she was definitely jealous of her own dog.

Oblivious to her irrational envy, man and dog snuggled their heads together in a long, heartfelt goodbye. Willow tried to tell herself that she was jealous because of how much Buddy obviously loved Caleb, but deep down, she knew it had more to do with Caleb's affection for the dog. Some lonely part of her heart craved some of that attention from him.

Clueless as to where her thoughts had gone, Caleb barely gave her a passing glance as he carried his duffel out the front door and said, "See ya Monday."

"Bye." She carefully kept her voice neutral, not wanting to let on that she was starting to have unwanted feelings for him.

Once Caleb was gone, she tried unsuccessfully to make small-talk with Mickey. "Anything sound good for dinner? I can have the chef make whatever you like."

"I already ate." He informed her curtly.

When Buddy went over and tried unsuccessfully to get the man's attention, her annoyance with him raised to new levels. *How could anyone ignore her sweet dog?*

She had to give Buddy credit because despite weekend after weekend of being shunned by the man, the dog remained ever-hopeful. He sat in front of Mickey and gazed up at him, non-verbally begging for a scratch or pat. Mickey kept his arms crossed and scanned the room as if the boogeyman was getting ready to jump out at them.

Willow knew it was his job to be on high-alert, but Caleb managed to do that, while still being a warm human being. In an effort to get the robot-like man to loosen up, she said, "I think Buddy is trying to get your attention."

Mickey's gaze darted down to the dog as if noticing him for the first time. He immediately went back to sweeping the room with his cold, beady eyes, but he said, "I'm not really a dog person."

"No kidding," Willow said under her breath. Since that was the most he had ever uttered to her at one time, she decided that he wasn't much of a people person either. Opting to keep that thought to herself, she said, "Sometimes, I forget Buddy is a dog."

The man paused his perusal of the room to quirk a brow in her direction, but he didn't comment.

Determined to get him to open up, she went on, "He's really quite sweet if you give him a chance. Caleb loves him to pieces."

Even though she only received a curt nod in response to her attempt to reach out, something urged her to go on. Smiling, she said, "In fact, Caleb has this hilarious thing he does where he grabs Buddy's paws and calls them his stompers, then pokes his teeth and calls them his chompers. It's really funny, and Buddy just loves the attention."

Even though she knew the man didn't appreciate her story, she chuckled at the memories. It felt good to talk to someone about Caleb's delightful relationship with her dog.

"Sounds to me like he needs to focus a little more on his job." Mickey finally weighed in.

Willow's hackles immediately rose. "Caleb is excellent at his job," she snapped, before flouncing off to her bedroom with Buddy on her heels.

Even though she knew the bodyguard would follow her and stand just outside the door, it felt good to walk away from him and shut her door with him on the other side. She refused to wonder why she suddenly felt so protective of the man charged with protecting her during the week.

Turning to look down at Buddy, she said, "Caleb is *not* getting under my skin."

For the first time since she'd brought him home, even her kindhearted dog looked skeptical of the truth in her words.

21

*T*he weekend seemed to drag on interminably. Willow tried to tell herself it was because she missed work--that she preferred to stay busy and try to keep her mind off the psycho that wanted to kill her and her lovable dog. Deep down, though, she knew that she was anxious for the shift change to happen with her bodyguards.

There was no denying that Caleb was more pleasant to have hanging around every moment of her days than Mickey was, but it was more than just his fun-loving personality that she missed during Mickey's shifts. Some undefined, simmering bubble of excitement from being around Caleb made her feel more alive when he was near. Being with Mickey just made her wish they would catch the criminal so she could go back to living a normal life, without constant surveillance.

She forced her tone to stay nonchalant when

she greeted Caleb on Monday morning. "Did you have a nice weekend?"

"It was great!" He enthused, which made Willow feel deflated.

She had spent the weekend moping around, counting the hours until Monday, while he was off having a 'great' time. She couldn't help but wonder if a woman had been the reason his time off was so great, but she knew that she didn't have any right to ask.

When he politely asked how hers was, she tried to drum up some enthusiasm when she responded, "It was fine."

"Just fine?" Caleb raised his brows, seeming honestly curious.

Deciding to reveal a bit of vulnerability, Willow said, "I'm just not as comfortable with Mickey as I am with you."

She could tell by the look on his face that her revelation had surprised him. Quickly masking it, he lightly teased her. "And here I thought you could barely stand having me around."

Not wanting to seem too desperate or clingy, she teased him right back. "Oh, that's true, but Mickey's even worse."

Proving how good-natured he was about her gentle ribbing, he tipped his head back and guffawed with laughter. She couldn't help but notice how white and straight his teeth were. His smile was practically made for television. She was pretty certain that it was completely natural, too... Unlike the veneers she had purchased as soon as she had been able to afford them.

Once his bout of laughter subsided, he said,

"Well, I guess I'm glad I'm not as bad to hang out with as an emotionless robot."

Willow's eyes opened wide in surprise. "You've noticed that, too? I thought maybe it was just me, but I can't get him to open up at all."

Caleb shook his head. "No, he's not exactly Mr. Personality, but he's good at his job. That's why I requested him as my weekend relief for you."

It was news to Willow that Caleb had requested Mickey for her. She couldn't keep the hope at bay that he might have arranged for the zero-personality fill-in as a way to make sure she didn't have a romantic connection with the weekend shift. As soon as the thought surfaced, she tried to quell it, knowing that it was probably just silly wishful thinking on her part.

Not wanting the silence to turn awkward, she revealed in a voice barely above a whisper, "He doesn't even like Buddy."

"What?!?" Caleb pretended to be scandalized as he bent down to talk directly to the dog. "How can this be? Hasn't he ever seen these wonderful floppies?"

Willow grinned down at the duo as Caleb rubbed his hands over Buddy's soft ears. *She couldn't be expected not to have warm feelings for a man who came up with such adorable and silly names for her dog's body parts, could she?*

Standing up and turning serious, Caleb said, "Ready to head to the studio? One more day of relative peace and quiet until the next letter arrives."

Willow's stomach immediately turned sour. It had been long enough that she was getting used to the new normal of having a 24-hour a day body-guard. It simply seemed like a part of her life, until she remembered the weekly letters and the maniac behind them.

Showing how intuitive he was to her feelings, Caleb said, "How about if we take Buddy to his favorite dog park by the water after the show tomorrow? We can walk back to your house along the cliff walk and look for whales. I saw some orcas breaching out in the distance there this weekend. It's really a sight to behold."

Willow hid the surge of disappointment she felt at hearing he had been that close to her house during the weekend and hadn't stopped by to see her. It shouldn't have surprised her. After all, who wanted to go to work on their day off? She had just secretly been hoping that she and Buddy were becoming more than just a job to him.

He was looking expectantly at her, awaiting her response to his suggestion. It was the first time he had made any activity recommendations to her. Normally, he simply followed along with whatever she had planned. Giving him a warm smile, she said honestly, "That sounds fantastic."

She reminded herself that it wasn't a date when the butterflies started fluttering their wings deep in her belly.

But when he grinned back at her and said, "Great... It's a date," those butterflies went into overdrive.

*C*aleb wondered if he had overstepped his bounds as Willow's bodyguard when he had suggested they go to the dog park and cliff walk, but he knew they would all three enjoy it. Willow hadn't seemed at all offended by the proposal. In fact, it almost sounded like she was looking forward to it.

He had noticed in his weeks with her that she was slowly beginning to come out of her shell. The irony wasn't lost on him that now that she was in real danger of being physically harmed by a crazed fan, she was beginning to go out in public without her hat and sunglasses disguises.

It felt marvelous that she trusted him to keep her safe, and he would do anything in his power to be worthy of her faith in him. He just hoped that once this maniac was caught and she no longer needed his services, that she would keep going outside for fresh air and not go back to her sheltered existence of shuttling back and forth between home and work only. That had to be a lonely way to live.

Smiling down at Buddy, he realized that the dog would probably take care of making sure she got out more. Although Caleb doubted if the golden retriever had a mean bone in his body, he might protect Willow if she was facing immediate danger.

When the letter arrived like clockwork on Tuesday, the now-familiar downcast expression returned immediately to Willow's face. Caleb hated it that she had to deal with this. No one should have to live in constant fear of being abducted or murdered––especially not a kind, generous, and fun-loving person, like Willow.

He smiled to himself as he realized that his initial impressions and prejudices regarding the celebrity had been way off base. Willow was truly one of the kindest people he had ever met. His worry that he might hesitate from saving her had been completely unfounded. He would gladly take a bullet for her or Buddy.

Seeing the worry cloud her normally vivid blue eyes made him say, "If you'll promise to stay in this dressing room, I'll call security down to watch the door, so you can stay in here rather than going to look at the latest letter."

He caught the flash of hope that sprang into her gaze before she tried to cover it with bravery. "No, I need to go see what it says."

"Actually, you don't. You know that someone is after you, and you know to be extra careful. I will tell you if anything changes or if we get any new clues, but I don't think it's necessary, or even healthy, for you to look at those letters every week."

She surprised him when she stood and hugged him to her. Other than a brief touch with her hand, it was the first warm gesture they had shared. It was beyond tempting to pull her closer and hold on, but he needed to maintain a professional distance.

When she whispered a sincere "thank you" near his ear, the tiny hairs on the back of his neck stood at attention. It was impossible to deny the spark of attraction he felt for this woman when she was so close to him.

Forcing himself to pull back, he gave her a curt nod and said, "Don't let *anyone* into this room while I'm away."

"Yes, sir." She mock-saluted him, but when he tilted his head in her direction, she nodded her compliance with his request.

Once the door was closed behind him, he muttered to himself, "She's gonna be the death of me."

After giving the building's security guard instructions not to let anyone through her dressing room door, he headed over to the elevator to go see this week's letter.

As he held up the note, he quickly realized there wasn't anything special about it. It was filled with threats and bad rhymes, just like all the others had been. They would send it to police forensics to see if they could gather any other clues, but it was starting to look like it might be another dead end.

He knew from experience that the criminal

would either slip up at some point or begin to escalate the threat. Eventually, sending scary letters wouldn't be enough of a high, and that is what Caleb needed to be prepared for.

Caleb knew his role would be to stand between the two celebrities and this lunatic, and he would gladly do it--no matter what it took. This is what he had trained for. He just had to force himself not to get too attached to the adorable duo. That could cloud his judgment or distract him, which wouldn't bode well for any of them.

Taking a deep breath to steel his resolve, he returned to Willow's dressing room. When he moved to knock on the door, the beefy security guard he had left there said in a gruff voice, "No one goes in."

Exasperated, Caleb said, "I didn't mean *me*. I'm their bodyguard." When the large guard continued to block the door with his arms crossed, Caleb said, "I'm the one who posted you here."

"No one goes in," the large man repeated.

"Willow!" Caleb yelled through the door past the over-eager security guard.

"Yes?" she asked, obviously standing near the door.

"It's Caleb. Let me in."

"I'm not supposed to let anyone in." Her voice had a lilting tone to it like she was immensely enjoying teasing him.

Rolling his eyes, he said, "That doesn't apply to me, and I think you know that."

Changing tactics, she asked through the closed door, "How do I know it's really you?"

After thinking it over for a moment, he

answered, "Let Buddy poke his snooping cone out here for a second. He'll confirm that it's really me."

Caleb enjoyed the throaty sound of her laughter at his silly answer.

When she opened the door a crack, Buddy stuck his nose out––almost like he knew what he was supposed to do. When she opened the door a little wider, Buddy came out with his tail almost hitting himself in the sides from wagging it so hard.

"Seems like he thinks you're safe," Willow gave Caleb a warm smile over the security guard's shoulder.

"Excuse me," Caleb said to the man, but he didn't budge until Willow put one of her dainty hands on his shoulder.

"It's okay, Bill," she assured the guard.

Bill finally moved to the side allowing Caleb access to the dressing room. As he walked in, Caleb firmly refused to think about how much it bothered him to see Willow's soft touch on the other man's broad shoulder.

*A*s much as Willow enjoyed filming her new show, which featured Buddy as the matchmaker extraordinaire, today she found herself looking forward to her final wink at the end of the show. She couldn't wait to go to the dog park and on a nice, relaxing walk with Buddy and Caleb.

Even though she tried to convince herself that she was looking forward to it so much because she knew her dog would love it, deep down, she knew that she was looking forward to spending some quality time with her handsome bodyguard. Despite how determined she had been not to like him, she found herself unable to keep from it.

She tried to hide her growing feelings for Caleb––even from herself––but they kept popping up at unexpected moments. The way he played with and smiled at her dog, his calm and reassuring presence, and his fun-loving easy sense of humor all combined to make him so attractive.

Even though he was impossibly gorgeous, too young for her, and off-limits due to his job, his magnetism was undeniable.

His job as her bodyguard made him practically irresistible. The fact that he would actually take a bullet for her was almost unfathomable, yet she truly believed that he would do it, if the need arose. That chivalry, coupled with the forbidden nature of a relationship with him made her secretly yearn for him even more. The more she tried to deny her feelings, the stronger they became.

As they rode in the car to the dog park, Buddy sat between them on the plush leather seat. They both absently stroked his soft fur, and the dog basked in the attention. When their hands lightly brushed against each other, their gazes darted together and quickly apart.

Willow yanked her arm back and folded her hands lightly in her lap. She wondered if he had felt the same zinging bolt of electricity as she had. Her strong attraction to Caleb was starting to concern her. It wouldn't serve her well to distract him from his job, but once the maniac was caught, Caleb wouldn't need to be with her anymore.

When she found herself wishing that it would take a while longer to catch her stalker, she realized how pathetic she had become. Not only did she have to hire people to hang out with her, but now she was hoping to lengthen the threat from a lunatic, just so she could spend more time with a man who thought of her merely as a frivolous celebrity. Pathetic didn't begin to cover how sad her lack of a love life had become.

When they reached the park, Willow forced those self-deprecating thoughts out of her mind. Just because Caleb was only with her because it was his job didn't mean that they couldn't have fun together. Maybe one of these days, he would begin to see her as more than just a spoiled diva. She knew she had much more than that to offer. She just needed to show some vulnerability and let him see the fun, relaxed, and humble sides to her personality.

As they walked with Buddy on his leash, Willow let the dog stop to sniff whatever caught his interest. He knew the way to the dog park entrance where they could set him loose, so she let him go at his own pace.

For his part, Caleb seemed content to meander at their sides. He seemed relaxed, but Willow noticed that his gaze was constantly scanning the horizon––most likely searching for anyone who could pose a threat.

When a mother and daughter approached them to request a selfie, Willow felt Caleb stiffen at her side. These two friendly faces obviously didn't pose a threat, but they still seemed to make him uncomfortable.

Once Willow and Buddy posed with them for some pictures and wished them a pleasant day, the trio moved on. Feeling bold, Willow hooked her arm through Caleb's elbow.

He paused for a moment to look down at her. Gently removing his arm, he said in a kind voice, "I have to be ready to act quickly if something should happen."

"Oh, right." Willow forced her lips into a smile,

hoping that her hurt feelings didn't show on her face. She had been foolish to think that Caleb might be starting to be attracted to her, too.

Feeling the need to say something else, she added, "I don't know what I was thinking."

"It's okay," Caleb assured her. "If I wasn't working, it would be fine."

"But you are working," Willow nodded, even as she reminded herself that she was 'just his job.'

When they reached the gate for the dog park, Willow went inside the enclosure with Buddy and unleashed him. He ran off at a high rate of speed in search of new friends. Before long, he was running, jumping, and playing with a standard poodle and a boxer.

Willow went back out the gate and stood beside Caleb to watch Buddy. "He really loves it here," she said as she watched her dog bounding around the park. When she looked at Caleb, she realized that he wasn't watching Buddy. Instead, he was scanning the park, in search of potential dangers.

"Don't you ever get tired of constantly being on high-alert?" She asked him, honestly curious.

"It's the job," he told her simply as if that explained everything.

"I know," she admitted before saying, "But you don't get to enjoy the little moments throughout your day."

"Most people don't enjoy their jobs. Although you obviously do." He smiled down at her for a moment before resuming his scanning.

It was silent for so long, Willow assumed they were done talking for a bit. He surprised her when he said, "Besides, who says I'm not enjoying myself?"

When her eyes darted to his to judge the sincerity of his semi-flirtatious comment, he was looking away, but his elbow brushed against hers as they leaned against the fence. She felt his warmth through her jacket and tried to remind herself that theirs was merely a professional relationship. It was becoming harder and harder to remember that.

They weren't lucky enough to glimpse any whales on the cliff walk as they trekked back to Willow's house, but Willow didn't mind. She was spending some quality time with two of her favorite men, and she couldn't imagine a better way to enjoy a crisp, sunny afternoon.

When the chilly breeze coming in to shore off the water began to kick up, Caleb gallantly offered her his leather jacket. She knew it would be in the best interest of her tender feelings to deny his chivalrous offer, but she couldn't resist. When he wrapped the soft leather around her shoulders, it was like being enveloped in his warmth.

She was tempted to lean her head down to sniff the shoulder of the jacket to see if it smelled like Caleb's signature scent of pine needles, Barbasol shaving cream, and a mysterious, yet marvelous, masculine odor that she couldn't quite put her finger on, but she forced herself to refrain from the desperate-looking maneuver.

It had been comfortably silent for so long, Willow felt somewhat startled when Caleb asked, "What's your real name, Willow Winks?"

She had been wondering what he was thinking about and was delighted to discover that his mind hadn't wandered to some woman from his 'real' life. Instead, he was curious about her. The realization was beyond thrilling.

"It's Willow Winks." She smiled up at him.

"No, I meant your given name. The one from your parents." Caleb obviously didn't believe her.

"That's really it." She promised him.

His mouth fell slightly open as he gawked down at her, clearly somewhat stunned. Confirming again, he asked, "Really?"

She couldn't help but laugh at the silly man before responding. "I wouldn't lie to you."

"Huh," he said, shaking his head before weighing in with his opinion. "I guess you really were destined for television."

Willow beamed at his approval. Shrugging her shoulders she said, "Guess so."

"And here I thought I was going to get the inside scoop on *THE* Willow Winks." Caleb teased her.

She grinned up at him, already knowing that he couldn't care less about her celebrity status. Turning serious, she asked, "What would you like to know?"

"Hmm." He scratched at his chin, pondering the question, and seeming to take it very seriously. Finally landing on something, he said, "Tell me something that no one else knows."

Willow thought about it for a long moment

before saying, "Okay, but you can't make fun of me."

"Would I ever?" He raised his shoulders in a 'Mr. Innocence' gesture.

"Yes." She laughed, but took a deep breath before revealing, "I read my horoscope every morning."

He gawked at her. "You believe in that ridiculous mumbo jumbo?"

Lightly shoving at his shoulder, she said, "You promised not to make fun of me."

"You're right." He admitted before amending his statement. "I meant to say that I find it intriguing that you believe in that hogwash." When she angled a narrowed gaze at him, he held up his palms and said, "Okay, okay... What did the stars predict would happen to you today?"

"That I would encounter a doubter and convince him that astrology is real," she quipped.

"Not likely," he answered.

She was well aware that most people considered horoscopes to be completely bogus, but she had always noticed a difference in her moods and emotions surrounding the cycles of the moon. More often than not, her daily horoscope held some nugget of truth in it. Even though it was usually generic enough to apply to almost anyone's day, she looked forward to reading it every morning.

Deep down, she realized it was silly, but she enjoyed the ritual nonetheless. Besides, why would she cut something out of her life that brought her pleasure? Feeling feisty, she asked him, "When is your birthday? I can tell a lot about you based on your sign."

Shaking his head in obvious disbelief that she took this so seriously, he answered with his sign rather than his birthdate. "I'm a Pisces."

She was surprised that he even knew his zodiac sign, but she didn't call him out on it. "Oh, no," she said, as she shook her head. "It's a good thing we aren't a couple."

"Why?" he asked, seeming truly curious, which made her heart thrum wildly in her chest.

"Because I'm a Libra. We would make a terrible match. Where I'm all about compromise, you tune into the needs of others."

"That sounds like a good match to me," Caleb decided, making her heart soar.

Trying to hide her body's reactions, she held up a finger and said, "You might think, BUT my sign is ruled by Venus and your sign is ruled by Neptune."

She could tell by his facial expression that she had lost him. "So?"

"So... I hate confrontation, and you have a tendency to be secretive. It's easy to see that we would implode before we really even had a chance to begin."

"Well, I guess it's a good thing we aren't romantically involved then," Caleb commented.

Nodding her agreement, she said, "Oh, for sure. But..." She inserted a dramatic paused and enjoyed seeing his eyes dart to hers.

"But?" he verbally nudged her.

"But if we were able to make it work as a couple, our intimacy levels would be off the charts." She felt her cheeks warm at the barely hidden innuendo of her words. It felt strange to be so forward with Caleb, but she was confident in her words.

Caleb seemed to be weighing her revelation in his mind. When he finally spoke, he surprised her by saying, "Off the charts, huh?"

At her nod, he simply said, "Wow."

25

*C*aleb never had trouble keeping his work life and personal life separate. He couldn't become overly attached to his charges. It might cloud his judgment at a critical moment, just as much as disliking them would. He was too good at his job to take that risk.

Willow Winks and Buddy were making it incredibly hard not to create a soft spot in his heart for them, though. When Willow had insinuated that their emotional intimacy levels would be sizzling if they had a romantic relationship, he was afraid his heart was going to beat right out of his chest. As loud as it was drumming in his ears, he was surprised Willow couldn't hear it.

He tried to play it cool, but he sensed that his feelings were as obvious as if they had been written across his face. There was no denying that Willow was attractive, but they were all wrong for each other. Besides, his sole focus needed to be on protecting her, not dating her.

When they reached the front door of her house, after their long walk, he did a quick perimeter check and found everything to be secure. Once they were safely inside, he said, "I'm kind of overheated from that walk up the hill, even though the wind off the water was chilly. Any chance you have some ice cream?"

The request was out of character for him. He normally just went along with whatever his charges wanted while he was working, but he had a real hankering for the frozen treat.

If Willow was surprised by his bold request, she didn't show it. She gave him a warm smile before saying, "I'm sure there's some in the freezer. Help yourself," she offered as she headed up to her bedroom.

Caleb made himself at home, getting out the ice cream scooper, two bowls, and two spoons. He imagined that Willow wouldn't allow herself to eat the mid-day treat, but he was going to make her some in the hopes that she would join him. Opening the massive, commercial-grade deep freezer, he dug around looking for something with chocolate.

"Don't you have anything besides peach?" he yelled up to towards her room.

He hadn't realized she was already on her way back downstairs, so her voice startled him when she answered. "Try the peach. I bet you'll like it."

"Mmn." The doubtful sound emerged from his throat, even as he pulled out a plastic container of peach ice cream.

Joining him to look down into the freezer, Willow pulled out a tray of frozen peach cobbler.

"I'll let this thaw out and we can have it after dinner, along with some fresh-brewed peach iced tea. You're going to love it," she added confidently.

He had his doubts about that, but he didn't voice his concerns. Instead, he asked, "What's with the peach fetish?"

Willow tipped her head back with a throaty laugh that made his breath catch. He wanted nothing more than to hear more of that delighted laugh, but he forced himself to focus on the wall just behind her ear. He couldn't let her know about the strong visceral reactions she caused in him when she let her guard down and revealed her true personality.

"I wouldn't call it a fetish," Willow lightly chastised him. "I do love peaches, though. But only Georgia peaches because they're the best... of course." She waved her hand as if that was a foregone conclusion before continuing. "I guess you can take the girl out of Georgia, but you can't take Georgia out of the girl. Peaches grown anywhere else––even here in the fantastic state of California––just don't taste quite right to me."

Her nose crinkled adorably as she talked about non-Georgia peaches. He was tempted to run his finger along those cute lines, so he focused on scooping out perfect globes of ice cream.

When he started to put some in the second bowl, she reacted exactly as he had predicted she would. "Oh, I really shouldn't have any."

She lightly patted her flat tummy as if that explained depriving herself of the treat she obviously loved. "We walked it off already," he easily shot down her protestation.

Holding up a full scoop to inspect it closer, he said, "Besides, if I have to taste ice cream with chunks of fruit in it, rather than chocolate--as God intended it, then you need to eat it too."

Nodding her agreement, she asked, "Shall we eat it outside on the deck, or is it too chilly for you?"

Her words seemed to hold a challenge. Never one to back down, he grinned and said, "I can handle it if you can."

They seemed almost like naughty children as they scurried out to the wraparound deck with stunning views of the ocean below. The breeze was colder than Caleb anticipated, especially with frigid bowls of ice cream in their hands, but he wasn't going to admit defeat. Instead, he offered to run inside for a blanket, which made Willow quickly nod her agreement.

When they settled onto the comfortable outdoor sofa, they snuggled close together to share the soft blanket he had retrieved. Buddy climbed up on the other side of Willow and rested his head in her lap.

She took a few bites of her ice cream before smiling up at Caleb and saying, "This is nice."

He was in full agreement, but he knew he was on a slippery slope where this intriguing woman and her lovable golden retriever were concerned. He stared out towards the inky blue sea and tried to convince himself that he should put some distance between them, even though that was the last thing he wanted.

Willow broke into his thoughts by asking, "Aren't you going to try your ice cream?"

Deciding that he had stalled long enough, he said, "Here goes nothing," as he looked down into the bowl before taking a tentative bite.

Willow was gazing up at him. Her bright blue eyes were filled when anticipation as she awaited his verdict. Evidently deciding it had been long enough, she prompted him. "Well??"

"Oh-my-gah," he mumbled around a second spoonful of the frozen manna from heaven. "So good."

After gracing him with a relieved, full-bodied laugh that carried out over the seaside cliffs, Willow rested her head lightly against his shoulder. It was a marvelous, relaxed moment that made Caleb realize his heart was a goner where this magnificent woman was concerned. He needed to pull back—or at least try to—for both of their sakes.

26

*C*harming and charismatic Willow Winks did not make it easy for Caleb to maintain a professional distance. He tried his best to ignore his undeniable attraction to her, but she was nothing like the spoiled, pretentious celebrity he had expected her to be. Instead, she was real, honest, and kind.

He inspected the wine bottle she had set out to go with the chicken and pasta dish her chef had left them for dinner. "Dorma Valley Wine is my favorite." He said, surprised that she had selected the reasonably-priced Chardonnay, rather than some overpriced, hoity-toity label.

"Mine too." She gave him an easy, warm smile as he uncorked the bottle and poured them each a glass.

It was starting to feel too much like a delightful date for Caleb's comfort level, so he tried to bring the conversation around to a work-related topic. "The police have been watching surveillance videos of the public mailboxes the letters were sent from, hoping to catch a glimpse of the person sending them."

Willow's spine straightened as if he had just thrown a glass of cold water on her, but she kept her tone even when she asked, "Have they had any luck?"

"Not really," Caleb admitted. "The letter sender's careful nature extends to mailing the letters, too. He or she wears a dark hood and mails the letters at night. The cops sent me the video clips, but it just looks like a shadowy figure. I'll let you watch them later, so you can see if you recognize anything. Maybe the shoes or body-type––although it's all pretty nondescript."

"Okay," she agreed before asking, "Can we not talk about this anymore tonight? I know I need to think about it and be on high-alert at work, but this is my safe space, and I don't want those frightening thoughts to intrude on me at home."

Caleb nodded, fully understanding her need to get away from the constant stress of knowing someone wanted to hurt her. "Of course. Besides, it's my job to make sure you're kept safe at all times, so let me do the worrying."

The fond smile she gave him could have melted a dish of peach ice cream in Antarctica. He returned it even as he realized he was failing miserably at being professional and aloof. This woman was wiggling her way into his carefully guarded heart.

While they ate, she asked him all kinds of personal questions. He normally refused to open up to his clients, as it wasn't his place, but he found himself gladly sharing details about his life.

When he told her about his violent hatred of seafood, she graced him with his favorite belly laugh. Loving the sound of it, he really laid it on thick. "I don't want to look at it, smell it, or even think about it… yuck!"

"You live on the coast, surrounded by fresh seafood restaurants. Most people would kill for the ocean fare options that are available along Cannery Row." She lightly chastised him, but she was smiling as she said it.

"I know… It's everywhere." He gave a mock-shiver of disgust, which made her giggle. Smiling, he added, "I guess I'm as bad as a person from Georgia who doesn't like peaches."

Pretending to be scandalized, she allowed her normally carefully controlled Southern belle accent to emerge when she dramatically fanned herself with her hand and said, "What? I do declare… That's pure blasphemy."

He couldn't help but chuckle at her antics. When she let her true personality shine through, she was nothing short of delightful.

When the conversation turned serious, he shared with her how his mother had worked tirelessly to raise him and his four sisters. He described each of his sisters and their varied personalities, as well as those of their children.

He knew his eyes lit up when he spoke about his nieces and nephews, but he couldn't help it. They were the lights of his life. He grinned conspiratorially at Willow before revealing, "My favorite thing to do is to play with them and get them all riled up before sending them home to their parents. I pride myself on being their 'cool' uncle."

The enamored way she looked at him when he spoke about his sisters' kids made warmth spread in his belly. He tried to tell himself that it was just friendly chatter between two people who were being forced to spend time together, but it felt like so much more than that.

She told him all about growing up as an only child, who had always longed for siblings. Giving him a sad smile, she added, "I would give anything to have a whole gaggle of nieces and nephews, like you do."

"You can borrow mine whenever you like," he said quickly, without thinking it through. He knew immediately that it was too intimate of a thing to say to his charge, but he loved the way her eyes lit up at the idea.

Unsure what came over him, he quickly went on. "I'm taking them ziplining next weekend at Pacific Adventure Amusement & Fun Center. You should come with us."

The invitation was out of his mouth before he thought it through. Considering the way her expression brightened before she said, "I'd love to," there was no way he could take it back now.

Seeming to sense that they had overstepped their professional boundaries, Willow quickly changed the subject. Walking over to stand beside the pre-heated oven and lifting the thawed pan of cobbler, she quipped, "Well, this peach cobbler isn't going to burn itself," as she slid it into the hot oven.

Her self-deprecating humor was just the tension breaker they needed after his awkward invitation. Smiling in her direction, he silently wondered how in the world he could be expected to continue to resist this enchanting woman.

Averting his gaze from her, he took a deep, centering breath and realized that he was in need of an icy cold shower to knock some sense back into his rebellious body. She was strictly off-limits. Maybe some frigid water would help him remember that.

27

*W*illow was surprised by Caleb's quick escape to his room after she put the cobbler in the oven to bake. She had thought they were having an easy-going, relaxing evening, and she had been thrilled by his impromptu invitation to go zip lining with him and his family.

Deciding that perhaps he was uncomfortable with the crumbling of his carefully erected walls that kept a professional distance between them, she curled up on the couch with her e-reader.

Never one to miss an opportunity to snuggle, Buddy climbed up beside her and circled himself into the crook of her knees. His warm body heat made all of the pent-up stress that she hadn't realized she was holding dissipate.

She absently rubbed the dog's soft fur with her left hand as she flicked through her book options with her right. Feeling the need for a sentimental, sweet book, she selected a heartwarming romance and settled in to read. If she wasn't meant to have a doting man in her life--other than Buddy--at least she could read about a romance heroine finding her soulmate.

The book must have been enthralling because the oven's buzzing timer startled her. She couldn't believe enough time had passed for the cobbler to bake.

Once she confirmed that the flaky crust was browned to perfection, she retrieved it from the oven and filled two bowls with the gooey peach and cinnamon treat. Uncertain if she should bother Caleb in his room, she decided to brew some hot herbal peach tea, rather than having iced tea. It was decaffeinated, so wouldn't affect their sleep, and it would complement their cobbler perfectly.

After the tea steeped, she sweetened it with cream and sugar. Once again, she was left to wonder if it would be overstepping her bounds to knock on Caleb's door. Deciding it would be rude not to, since the tea was hot and the cobbler was warm, she made a slam decision to deliver the mug to him. She didn't figure he would want to eat in his room, so she left the cobbler on the counter.

Standing outside the closed door, she almost chickened out. Deciding it was her house and that she was being silly, she rapped her knuckles on the door. "Caleb?"

"Yeah?" His voice sounded muffled through the door.

Turning the handle with her free hand, she

said, "I brought you some hot tea, and the cobbler's..."

Her voice trailed off at the end because Caleb was standing in the middle of his room wearing only a towel around his waist. His dark hair was damp, obviously from a recent shower. She watched, mesmerized, as a drop of water trailed down his firm tummy.

She knew she should avert her gaze, but some unknown instinct compelled her to drink in the sight before her. When she swallowed, it felt so loud that she was certain he could hear it across the room.

They stayed frozen like that for a long moment. Finally, realizing that she was intruding on his privacy, she mumbled, "Sorry... I just... Here's tea... And the cobbler is ready."

She knew she was rambling, but she couldn't seem to form coherent sentences. She was too distracted by the towel and his broad, strong shoulders that tapered down into an intriguing vee at his waist. He was physical perfection. Some logical part of her brain knew that she shouldn't stare, but her misbehaving eyes would not comply with her mind's demand to look away.

"I'll be right down. Thanks." He said, effectively dismissing her.

His words seemed to knock some sense into her. She whirled around to leave, but she moved too fast and some of the hot liquid sloshed out over her hand. The shock of being burned startled her so much that she dropped the ceramic mug. It fell onto the cherry hardwood floor and shattered into pieces.

Bending down, her immediate reaction was to say, "I'm sorry."

Caleb's calm, soothing voice came from right behind her. The hair on the back of her neck stood on end as she realized how close he must be to her. She was acutely aware of how little he was wearing. "Are you okay? Did you get burned?"

"I'm fine, but I broke my favorite mug," she mumbled, embarrassed that merely seeing a man covered by a towel could make her act like such a bumbling fool. "I'll get this cleaned up."

"Don't worry about it," he offered kindly. "I'll take care of it. Why don't you go run some cool water on your hand and check your first aid kit for some burn cream?"

It dawned on her then that he had bare feet. "Don't step on the glass," she warned him.

"Stop worrying about me and go take care of your hand," he ordered her firmly.

Something about his no-nonsense tone made her obey, despite the fact that she didn't want to leave him with her mess.

As she obediently ran cool water from the kitchen faucet over the angry red skin on her hand, she thought about how silly she had been. Caleb was a gorgeous, kind-hearted man in the prime of his life. What on earth would he see in an aging, lonely celebrity?

She knew he didn't care a bit about her fame or her fortune. Those superficial benefits of success didn't impress him. If anything, he found them to be off-putting. Caleb was a salt-of-the-earth, rugged outdoorsman, and it was time she faced the fact that he only spent any time with her because he was being paid to do so.

After she opened her first aid kit and rummaged around in it, she found some burn relief cooling gel, gauze, and a bandage. When the tiny hairs on her arm tingled and stood at attention, she sensed that Caleb had joined her in the kitchen. As much as she wanted to protect her fragile feelings, her wildly thumping heart at his nearness told her that her hired protector might actually turn out to be the most dangerous threat to her emotional well-being.

2 8

*S*he felt Caleb standing directly behind her. When he whispered near her ear, "Let me see your hand," her spine stiffened as a delicious chill raced along it.

Turning, she obliged by holding her hand up for his inspection.

He took his time as he gingerly applied the cooling gel for her. He covered the entire area with a light coating before saying, "I don't think it's going to leave any scarring, but we can head over to the med center, if you'd like to have it checked out by a doctor."

She was already shaking her head before he had the offer completed. "No, it's not a big deal. I'm just a clumsy, old fool." When his eyes darted to hers, she quickly continued, not wanting him to think she was fishing for compliments. "I'm sure it will heal in no time."

"I think it will, too," he assured her before

adding, "But you are not clumsy, old, or a fool. Everyone drops things occasionally."

He gently placed a sterile pad over the affected area to lock in the healing gel. Then he securely wrapped a gauze bandage around her thumb to hold it in place.

When he finished with his kind ministrations he kept her hand within his. "All better?"

She nodded, uncertain of her voice. He was being too caring and wonderful. She didn't want to reveal her budding romantic feelings for him, but she feared she wouldn't be able to mask them if she spoke.

"My mom used to always kiss my boo-boos to make them feel better," he revealed, looking down at her bandaged hand.

When his eyes met hers, she felt her breath hitch in her throat. Her voice sounded croaky when she asked, "Did it work?"

"Absolutely," he answered, grinning down at her.

"My mom wasn't that maternal," she told him. Knowing she was playing a dangerous game, but unable to stop herself, she added, "I've never had anyone to kiss my boo-boos."

The heavy-handed hint hung for a long moment in the air between them. They were separated by mere inches as he continued to gingerly hold her injured hand with his. Caleb seemed to be carefully weighing his options.

Just when she thought he was going to turn away, he surprised her by lifting her hand higher and pressing his lips to the bare skin right next to her bandage.

Her hand felt fully alive from his kiss. The warm pressure of his lips made heat emanate out from the spot where they were connected. She closed her eyes, savoring his touch. The ridiculous thought that she might never wash that spot on her hand again surged into her brain.

Too soon, he pulled back.

Willow asked him the first question that popped into her mind. "Would you really take a bullet for me?"

"Absolutely," he answered without hesitation.

Willow thought she might melt into a deliriously happy puddle. The idea that this glorious man would risk his life for her made her feel sheltered and secure.

His eyes were as smooth and dreamy looking as melted milk chocolate as he gazed down at her. They stood there like that for a long moment, drinking each other in and breathing heavily from their close proximity.

Willow thought he might kiss her on the mouth. She tilted her head up slightly and flicked her tongue out to wet her lips, wanting to be ready.

He watched her, seeming mesmerized before he leaned down, putting his lips mere inches from hers. When he froze, he seemed to be pondering the monumental moment.

They remained suspended like that--so close, yet so far away. Willow was tempted to tip up onto her toes to close the gap between their mouths, but she sensed that Caleb was fighting an internal battle. She didn't want to make the decision for him.

When he finally pulled back, she immediately wished that she had been more forward. His decision to not kiss her left her aching for more. She wanted to feel his soft lips brush against hers, and she had missed what would likely be her only opportunity.

Caleb didn't let his carefully constructed walls down often, and she feared she had just flubbed a once-in-a-lifetime opportunity with him.

He ran a hand through his thick hair and said, "I'm sorry. I shouldn't have let my feelings get in the way. We can't be a couple."

After he shoved off the counter and headed towards his bedroom, Willow blew a long breath from her mouth. As much as she didn't want to distract him from his job, which was vital to her well-being, it was wonderful to know that he was attracted to her––at least on some level.

Now, the challenge would be to find a way to break through that chink in his armor, without endangering their safety.

Despite the threat hanging over her head, and the fact that Caleb had just verbally reaffirmed his commitment not to have a personal relationship with her, Willow suddenly felt a renewed hope for her pathetically lacking romantic life.

29

*C*aleb paced in his room like a caged animal, silently berating himself for allowing Willow and her lovable pooch to so thoroughly get under his skin. He had never before overstepped the bounds of a strictly professional relationship with any of his charges, and he couldn't quite wrap his head around the fact that he was beginning to care for Willow and Buddy-- way too much.

His inappropriate feelings for them could cloud his judgment or keep him from reacting quickly enough to a physical threat to their safety. Ironically, the more he cared about them, the more danger he put them in because he wouldn't be able to look at their situation and surroundings like an outside, unbiased observer.

Having feelings for his charges made him vulnerable and put the ones he was protecting in danger. He couldn't abide by that.

As he paced, he tried to determine if he should

quit his job as their bodyguard and find a suitable replacement. That prospect wasn't overly appealing. After all, whom could he find that he would trust to take care of them? It was almost all he could do to leave them with Mickey on the weekends, and Mickey was practically a bodyguard robot.

Since he couldn't stand to entrust their safety to anyone else, he decided that he would just need to keep his distance and control his personal feelings, until the threat was eliminated.

Willow and Buddy's safety was his top priority, which meant that he couldn't risk losing any focus from his job. His growing feelings for them were a distraction that needed to be eliminated. From now on, he would be all-business, all the time.

He would just have to ignore how lovely Willow's hair looked glistening in the sunlight, how her deep laugher made his stomach tighten, and how her sparkling blue gaze caused his heart to skip a beat.

Shaking his head in frustration, he ran his fingers through his dark brown hair. He was a goner where this woman was concerned. It would probably be best for all concerned if he distanced himself from Willow and Buddy and stepped back from his job as their protector. That was the last thing he wanted to do, though.

In the weeks he had spent with Willow, he had grown to enjoy their easy camaraderie, their silly banter, and that undeniable spark of romantic attraction that sizzled just beneath the surface of all of their interactions.

Flopping down flat on his back on his bed and

crossing his hands behind his head, he decided that he wasn't ready--or likely able--to let them go just yet. Rather than putting their safety at risk, he would just have to renew his laser focus on catching the lunatic that was threatening them.

Maybe he could enjoy Willow's sparkling and vivacious personality once his job was complete, if she would have him; but until then, he was the only person standing between them and a homicidal maniac. He needed to be ready at all times to protect them, and that meant ignoring his ever-growing attraction for Willow.

He knew it wouldn't be easy to shift their relationship back to a strictly professional one, but he could be a stubborn stickler when he needed to do so. He just hoped that Willow would understand the abrupt change in his demeanor.

The next morning, he joined her at breakfast after a thorough check of the perimeter of the house. They normally watched the early-morning news program together on the small flat-screen in her kitchen while they ate fresh croissants with fruit jam. She sipped her tea, while he drank his coffee, and they shared the newspaper--an actual print version of it.

They both normally relaxed and enjoyed their quiet morning time together, but today Caleb was determined to make sure she knew he was there only to do his job.

He looked through her to the shimmery beige wall behind her when he said, "I've allowed security to get a little lax around here."

Ignoring the scoffing sound she made in her throat that was obviously intended to let him know she believed he was doing a good job, he continued in a monotone voice. "All of our chit-chatting and socializing distracts me from my job, so we need to scale the friendliness back... all the way back... so I can remain focused on what is important."

He did his best not to notice the hurt look that darkened her normally bright blue eyes. Instead, he averted his gaze once more and said flatly, "We're not friends. I'm here to ensure your safety. That's all."

He didn't have to look at her eyes to know that they had turned stormy with anger at his rude brush-off of their budding friendship and undeniable spark of romantic attraction. When she said crisply, "Understood," he knew his harsh words had hit their mark.

As hard as it was to hurt her feelings like this, it was much easier than it would be to know he had let her down when she was counting on him to keep her safe. She needed to know that her safety was his top priority... his only priority. Nothing else mattered.

illow was beyond hurt by the sudden shift in Caleb's attitude. He went from being charming and fun-loving to acting like more of a robo-bodyguard than Mickey. She'd never had a moment of doubt that Caleb would keep her safe, even when he allowed his tightly-held control of his feelings to slip, so she wasn't sure why he had suddenly clammed up.

When she joked with him or tried to get him to open up, he stared through her... almost like she wasn't a real person. After having experienced the full sunlight of his warm gaze on her the past few weeks, it felt like she had suddenly been shoved outside at the North Pole without so much as a light jacket to protect her from the bitter cold.

While she appreciated his commitment to his job, she missed their fun interactions. She saw no reason why he couldn't keep her safe and be an actual human being with feelings and a live heart beating in his chest. If that softer, gentler side of him wished to explore a more-than-friends relationship with her, then she was willing to see where things went.

When the time came for the normal changing of the guards, she wasn't about to let him off the hook without firming up the plans for the invitation he had extended prior to his change of heart about the appropriateness of their growing friendship.

She watched for a long moment as Caleb and Mickey spoke to each other in monotone voices. Buddy nudged Caleb's hand, practically begging for some attention, but the man merely gave him a swift pat on the head before pointing out some mysterious weak area in the fence line that Mickey needed to be aware of.

Having already experienced Mickey's lack of interest in giving him any attention, Buddy reluctantly flopped down. Willow hated to see the dejected look in the dog's sweet brown eyes. She was fairly certain that same look emerged in her eyes when Caleb ignored her attempts to get his attention.

Deciding not to let him get away with ignoring her, she asked boldly, "What time are we taking your nieces and nephews zip lining tomorrow?"

He looked surprised by the question as if he had completely forgotten inviting her to come along. It had happened back when they were friends, but that was no reason for him to assume she was no longer coming.

His feelings for her might have dissipated, but hers for him were just as strong as ever. If anything, they had grown more intense at his refusal to acknowledge that they had anything more than a professional relationship. Apparently, the old adage about wanting what you can't have was accurate. The fact that Caleb was trying to deny that they had any chemistry drove her crazy.

"Oh, right." He rubbed a hand along the back of his neck as if he was trying to think of a way to get out of the commitment to her without being overly rude.

Refusing to back down, she merely raised her brows in his direction. Not long ago she would have been self-conscious about him obviously wishing to rescind the offer. She likely would have made up an excuse about having forgotten she had other plans that she couldn't cancel, but something about Caleb made her want to challenge his resistance to growing closer to her.

"I won't be able to keep a proper eye on you with all of the kids around," he tried.

"It's okay," she smiled sweetly before reminding him, "It's the weekend, so Mickey will be there to watch over me." She turned her smile to the other bodyguard. Both men stared at her with blank faces. Mickey's had suddenly gone pale.

"On a zipline, ma'am? I don't like heights." He actually sounded nervous. It was the first chink he had ever shown in his tough-man armor.

Mickey was starting to look like he might be ill just from the thought of climbing up to zipline, so she quickly let him off the hook. "I think you'll be able to keep an eye on things just fine from the ground. Besides, Caleb will be up top with me, right?"

She had him backed into a corner, so he had no choice but to agree. "Yes, I'll make sure she stays safe while we're up there."

"Great! It's settled then. What time should we meet you at the adventure center tomorrow morning?" She wasn't going to give him the opportunity to weasel out of their plans.

Shaking his head, Caleb said, "We'll meet you by the go carts at 10."

"Can't wait." She beamed a smile in his direction.

Evidently accepting that this was happening, despite his recent decision to distance himself from Willow, he said, "I hope you like kids because my nieces and nephews are handfuls."

Willow hadn't spent much time with kids during her adult life, but she decided to go with the adage that had seen her through many uncertain times in her life--fake it until you make it. Infusing her voice with confidence, she said, "I love children."

Both men bugged their eyes out at her, but neither was brave enough to call her out on the lie.

*W*illow stared with glassy eyes at the letter Mickey had just placed in front of her on her granite kitchen counter. It had the same meticulously cut-and-glued letters and ridiculous rhymes as the previous letters, so it was obviously from the same person; but in many ways it was different than the previous threats.

The most frightening change was that this letter had been delivered in-person to her home. That meant this crazy person knew where she lived. That realization made Willow shiver as if ice water was making its way through her veins.

This letter had also broken the pattern by arriving on Saturday. The previous notes had arrived like clockwork every Tuesday morning. That had become her new normal. Although they were frightening, the threats were also steady and predictable.

This note had come early, which indicated things were escalating. Instead of following the weekly routine or even losing interest in threatening her and Buddy, the maniac was stepping up the hate-filled warnings to higher levels.

"This is very concerning. This person knows where you live and he or she is no longer getting a thrill from the weekly threats sent to the studio. They are starting to need more to get the same high. Soon, the notes won't be enough, and he'll try to get to you in person." Mickey's voice betrayed no emotion, despite how dire his prediction was.

"I know." Willow snapped, not appreciating how flippantly Mickey mentioned her being in grave danger. Feeling the need to deal with this rationally, rather than let her emotions take over, Willow suggested, "We need to watch the security cameras' video footage to see if we can identify who delivered this."

Mickey deflated her sails by saying, "I already watched the videos. This person is cagey. I didn't see more than a shadowed, hooded figure on the footage."

"We should still send it to the police," Willow suggested, hoping they might see something Mickey missed.

"I already did," he reassured her.

As he hovered awkwardly behind her, Willow couldn't help but wonder how Caleb would react to the heightened threat. Before his renewed determination to keep his distance from her, he would have placed a comforting hand on her shoulder, and it would have made her feel better. Now, he might be just as aloof as Mickey.

Taking a deep, centering breath, she asked

Mickey, "Are you ready to head out to the amusement center?"

Mickey's face screwed up in surprise when he asked, "You still want to do that? You would be much more secure here where I can keep a close eye on you, rather than out in the open outdoors."

"I'm not going to let this maniac run my life." She retorted firmly. "If I hide inside all the time, that lets him win, right?"

She wasn't really expecting an answer to her question, and Mickey didn't give her one. He seemed to be mentally calculating the logistics of keeping her safe in such a public setting. His brow was furrowed into even deeper lines than normal.

Knowing that he was only concerned for her safety, she tried to make him feel better. "We'll keep it low-key. I won't do any social media posting until we are safely back home. Besides, Caleb will be there, so I should be doubly-safe."

She smiled in Mickey's direction, but he didn't look in the slightest bit amused. Not giving him the chance to try to talk her out of it, she said, "Let's go." As an afterthought, she added, "And we are NOT telling Caleb about this new letter. It's his day off. We'll tell him about it when he gets to work on Monday morning."

Mickey looked uncertain about keeping this from the other bodyguard, so Willow gave him a firm look to remind him who was paying his salary. She silently reminded herself that technically the studio was paying him, but when he nodded his agreement, she knew that he understood that she was the one in charge.

"Let's go zipline." Mickey didn't even try to

insert a tiny bit of enthusiasm into his voice, which made Willow chuckle.

Reaching up to put her arm around his stiff, straight shoulders she said, "You never know, Mick… you might actually like it."

"I can promise you I won't, ma'am."

"We'll see about that," she teased him as they headed out for the car, even though she knew without a doubt that he would not, in fact, enjoy himself.

Once they were settled in the car with Buddy flopped between them on the leather seat, the rigid bodyguard looked out the window as he said to her, "Please don't call me Mick. I don't believe in nicknames."

Something about that struck her as funny. He gave her a questioning look as if he couldn't comprehend what she was laughing at, which made her laugh even harder.

He continued to glare at her, and she realized that her laughter might have hurt his feelings——if he had any. Turning serious, she said, "I'm sorry. It won't happen again."

"See that it doesn't," he said tersely.

Willow was a bit taken aback until she saw the corner of his lip turn up ever-so-slightly. Smiling and shaking her head, she realized that her weekend bodyguard might have a tiny sliver of a personality hidden somewhere deep inside his barrel-sized chest.

She blinked and the hint of a smile was gone. She was left wondering if she had imagined it as she absently rubbed Buddy's head, which was resting on her leg.

*T*heir arrival at the fun center was anything but discrete. When Nico pulled the SUV to a stop in front of the entrance gate, Caleb and a whole gaggle of kids were standing in line to purchase tickets to get inside.

As soon as Buddy jumped out of the car, the kids all ran to greet him. Caleb gave up his spot in line to join them. They created such a spectacle as the kids went crazy over the happy dog. It wasn't long until a crowd gathered around them.

Willow posed for pictures and signed autographs. Buddy happily lapped up the attention from the kids and seemed like he smiled on cue when fans wanted to snap a picture of him.

After the crowd finally dispersed, Willow noticed the short, blonde woman standing near Caleb. She was adorable and closer to Caleb's age than Willow was. Willow didn't like the surge of jealousy she felt when she saw the other woman place a possessive hand on Caleb's shoulder. She was a firm believer that women needed to stick together, and she didn't like her brand-new envious streak one bit.

Willow silently berated herself for forcefully inserting herself into Caleb's day. He obviously had a date and hadn't had the heart to tell her she couldn't join them. He probably thought she was a lonely, pathetic loser, so his kind heart wouldn't let him hurt her feelings.

The tiny woman looked up at Caleb and said, "Aren't you going to introduce me to her, princess?"

Willow did a double-take. *Had this tiny firecracker just called Caleb princess?* Several of the kids covered their mouths with their hands as they attempted to hide the fact that they were laughing, which led Willow to believe that she had heard her correctly.

Caleb's dark brows slashed into a decidedly perturbed vee. "Really, Cassidy? I thought we agreed you wouldn't call me that in front of the kids."

Something about the woman's name was familiar, but it took Willow a long moment to place it. As soon as Cassidy beamed a smile up at Caleb, recognition dawned on Willow. Cassidy's ornery grin perfectly echoed her older brother's. The envy immediately dissipated as she realized this woman was Caleb's youngest sister.

Evidently losing patience with her brother, Cassidy extended her hand out towards Willow. "Hi, Willow. I'm Caleb's favorite sister, Cassidy."

"Hardly," Caleb rolled his eyes dramatically.

His over the top reaction made Willow think the assertion might be true. "She's my *baby* sister."

Cassidy ignored his attempt to rile her up. Instead she gave Willow a warm smile. "Caleb and I are the only two siblings without kids, so we take all of these rugrats a Saturday or two a month and give their parents a day off."

"I bet they appreciate that." Willow smiled as she looked around at the stair-stepping heights of the rather large group of children.

When her eyes landed back on Cassidy, she was surprised that she hadn't noticed the family resemblance with Caleb when she first saw the woman. Caleb's youngest sister was like a miniature feminine version of him. It was uncanny. She even had his warm brown eyes, but they seemed to sparkle with an extra hint of mischief.

Reaching up to sling her arm around Willow, Cassidy said, "So, tell me how you managed to get through my brother's thick skull that it's okay for him to have a little bit of fun with someone he's watching. He's never brought anyone he worked for around us before."

Willow felt a thrill race down her spine at the thought that she might be special to Caleb, but she immediately tamped it down by reminding herself that she had practically insisted on it. She liked Cassidy, though, and wanted to encourage the woman's warm welcoming embrace, so she leaned in conspiratorially and said, "I'm still working on getting through that thick skull."

It must have been the right thing to say because Cassidy tipped her head back and hooted with loud laughter before saying, "I think you and I are going to get along just fine, Willow Winks."

With that, the two women headed arm-in-arm towards the park's entrance. Mickey stayed close behind the ladies, which left Caleb to corral the kids on his own.

Once inside the fun park, the kids went crazy––each one was begging to go in a different direction. It got so hectic that Caleb raised his fingers up to his lips and let out a piercing whistle. That gesture got everyone's attention.

In a firm voice, Caleb said, "We're here to zipline, so we're doing that first. If that goes well, we'll discuss the possibility of doing more activities."

He let the threat hang in the air that if it didn't go well, there definitely wouldn't be any further fun at the amusement park. The children's large eyes blinked up at him, seeming to hang on his every word.

Willow couldn't help but be impressed with how easily he managed to wrangle the rowdy brood and get them to behave. It dawned on her then what a fantastic father he would make. She found herself smiling as she wondered what a tiny version of Caleb would look like. His son's appearance probably wouldn't be too far removed from the little boys in this group.

Caleb had gotten everyone's attention and laid down the law, so Cassidy took it upon herself to play 'good cop' by yelling, "Let's go zipline!"

She charged off in the direction the colorful map indicated with the excited group of kids following closely in her wake.

Willow, Caleb, and Mickey held back a moment, which prompted Cassidy to turn back to yell at her brother, "You coming, princess?"

Caleb scowled at the nickname, before turning to Willow to say, "Be glad you don't have any siblings."

Willow chuckled as they moved to follow Cassidy and the kids. She nodded to acknowledge his sentiment, but she was thinking that even if they picked on her relentlessly, having several siblings would be a dream come true.

*W*illow felt like she needed to take notes as she listened to the teenager ramble off the safety instructions for their zip lining adventure. The young man had obviously made the spiel many times before. He spoke very fast, and his monotone voice made him nearly impossible to understand.

She tried to lean in to better see and hear what he was saying, but she still feared she had missed something important. The others in the group were whispering excitedly among themselves and not paying a bit of attention. She felt the urge to yell at them that this was important, but she didn't want to come off as a total jerk.

Mickey had offered to stay on the ground on this end of the line to keep Buddy safe. It was tempting to stay on solid earth with them, but she didn't want to look like a chicken.

Once their brief training was done, the young man asked who would like to go first. Willow took a step back, but all of the kids raised their hands enthusiastically.

Cassidy suggested, "Let's have Uncle Caleb go first, so he'll be there to catch everyone on the other end."

Willow liked the sound of that, but she tried not to let the anticipation show on her face. Having Caleb's open arms waiting for her was about the only thing that would make this crazy stunt worthwhile.

The kids let out a collective groan at not being chosen to go first, but they quickly rallied when Caleb said, "I'll go first to make sure it actually goes all the way to the other end."

Before long, Caleb was fitted with a helmet and strapped into the harness. Willow held her breath and squeezed her eyes shut as he started traveling the line, hanging from an impossibly thin cable. When she heard him yell, she peeked one eye open and was thrilled to see that he was zooming through the air. In fact, he was holding an arm out as if he was relaxed and having a blast.

Once he was safely on the other side, the kids scrambled and begged to be next. One by one Cassidy selected them and sent them on their way.

When only one child was left, the little girl blinked up at Cassidy and asked, "Why did you pick me last, Aunt Cass? Does that mean you like me the least?"

Cassidy leaned down and said, "No, sweet Ella. I picked you last because I like you the most."

When the little girl gave her a confused look, Cassidy said, "You still have your ride to look forward to, but the others are all already finished with theirs. Plus, I got to hang out with you the longest."

The little girl beamed with pride, when she asked, "So you like me the bestest, and I'm your favoritest?"

Cassidy leaned down to whisper near the child's ear, "Yes, but don't tell the others."

"I won't," Ella promised solemnly. Her cornflower-blue eyes sparkled with sincerity.

Willow couldn't help but smile at the sweet interaction. Cassidy was obviously great with kids. Her handsome brother was, too.

How was a lonely, aging celebrity supposed to resist this charming, rambunctious family? Willow wanted to be included in their family fold so badly she could practically taste it.

Ella squealed with glee as she sailed along the zipline. Once she safely reached the other side, Cassidy turned to face Willow. "I guess we're the final two. Would you like to go first or after me?"

Fearing she might chicken out if she was left on the platform alone with the pimply-faced assistant, Willow took a deep breath and said, "I'll go next."

Once she was attached to the line, she pulled obsessively at the straps to make sure they were secure. It didn't feel like she had nearly enough holding her on the cord, and she couldn't even stand to look at how thin the line itself looked. It felt like she was entrusting her safety to a flimsy laundry line that might break at any moment.

Willow allowed the attendant to perform his minimalistic safety checks and before she knew it, she was flying through the air at a high rate of speed. She opened her mouth, but no sound came out. She sailed down the slope, high over the tree-tops of the redwood forest canopy, feeling weightless.

The temptation was strong to squeeze her eyes shut, but this was the first time in longer than she cared to admit that she had done anything even remotely daring, and she wanted to remember every moment.

When her gaze travelled to the end of the line, she saw Caleb there waiting for her. Suddenly, she felt safe. Even though it was illogical to think that Caleb would be able to stop her from falling from so far away, she felt confident that he wouldn't let anything happen to her.

They locked eyes as she sailed through the air towards the platform he was waiting on. There was no denying the warm look in his gaze as he watched her. She longed to have that adoring look from him always, but she feared that he would go back to his guarded, aloof expression as soon as they were both back on solid ground.

Deciding to enjoy it while it lasted, she stared at him as she neared the end of the line. Suddenly, she began to wonder how she was supposed to stop this blasted ride. The last thing she wanted was to show her ignorance by being the only one to go flailing into the tree beyond the end of the line, like a ridiculous cartoon character.

Just as panic was beginning to set in, she miraculously began to slow. Caleb spread his arms wide open as he waited for her to touch down on the platform. That warm welcome was enough to quell Willow's rising bubble of panic.

It had dawned on her as she barreled towards him that she would walk over hot coals, if Caleb was waiting to embrace her on the other end. The realization was both thrilling and frightening.

He easily caught her in his arms to help soften her landing on the platform. They stood there holding each other for a long moment. Willow was breathing heavily both from the thrill of the zipline and from being so close to Caleb. She could easily get addicted to the warm, sweet look he was giving her.

The line attendant, who looked to be a couple of years older than the young man on the other end, stepped forward to help disconnect Willow from the harness. Caleb held up a hand to stop him as he said, "I'll help her."

Once she was free, they stood there together gazing at each other for longer than was probably socially acceptable. It wasn't until they heard Cassidy's high-pitched screeching as she zipped in their direction that the spell was finally broken.

Caleb reluctantly let go of Willow as they moved out of the way for Cassidy's landing. The tiny woman sailed gracefully onto the platform as if she had done this a million times, but she glared in her brother's direction. "Don't bother to help me. I'm only your favorite sister."

"I knew you had it under control." He gave her an exasperated look.

Ella blinked up at them, looking perplexed, before accusing Caleb, "I thought my mom was your favorite sister."

"Shh... Aunt Cassidy doesn't know that." He

lifted a finger to his lips as if the little girl was giving away a big secret.

Cassidy opened her eyes wide in pretend outrage at her brother as the flustered young attendant attempted to unhook the beautiful, feisty woman. "What? You mean I'm not your favorite? How can this be?!?"

Caleb pulled his sister into a loose bear hug. "Of course you're my favorite sibling," he assured her loudly while vehemently shaking his head past her shoulder to deny his words to the children standing behind her.

The kids were all giggling with glee at their aunt and uncle's over-the-top, dramatics. Willow couldn't help smiling along with them, unaccustomed to the silly siblings' antics.

Pulling back, Cassidy pretended like she didn't know what Caleb had done behind her back. "That's more like it. I'm ready for ice cream. Who is with me?"

The kids let out a collective shout as Caleb led the way down from the platform. Cassidy slung a friendly arm around Willow's shoulders and said conspiratorially, "I like to get them all sugared-up before sending them home to their moms."

Willow couldn't help but laugh at the spirited woman. She was quickly discovering that Cassidy was just as delightful and likable as her brother. She couldn't help but wonder if the rest of his sisters were as open and friendly as Cassidy. It was surprising to discover that she desperately wanted to find out.

The rest of their time together at the amusement center went by in a marvelous, but too-fast blur. The ice cream was delicious. They even got a pup-sized vanilla version for Buddy, which he happily lapped up.

They rode bumper cars and go-carts. The kids played arcade games. Caleb won a goldfish for Ella, which had Cassidy hooting with laughter over what their oldest sister's reaction would be to that unwelcome addition to their family.

When they finally sat down to share a couple of big, greasy, and gooey pizzas, Willow couldn't quite believe how much fun the day had been.

Mickey stood stiffly behind their table with his arms crossed as if watching them enjoy the day annoyed him to no end.

Cassidy leaned over to whisper in Willow's ear as she thumbed the large, aloof man. "He's a barrel of laughs. Is Caleb like that when he's on duty?"

Willow smiled over at Caleb as she watched

him wipe an orange grease stain off his youngest nephew's cheek. "Caleb takes his job very seriously," she told his sister before adding, "But he knows how to have fun, too."

"Reeeallly?" His sister asked, raising her eyebrows in Willow's direction. Evidently something in Willow's tone had piqued Cassidy's interest.

Wanting to curb this line of questioning before Cassidy embarrassed Caleb, Willow toned down her response. "He draws the line at having a relationship with anyone he's guarding."

Cassidy tilted her chin in Willow's direction before asking quietly, "Would you be open to having a romantic relationship with him, if he wasn't your bodyguard?"

Willow was caught off-guard by the direct question. She had just met Cassidy, but she was already beginning to feel like they were friends. She reminded herself that this woman was Caleb's sister, so anything she said would likely make its way directly to his ears. Even though her initial instinct had been to respond in the affirmative, she instead said, "Perhaps."

"Hmm." Cassidy grinned in her direction. It was obvious the wheels were already turning in her mind, and Willow decided it wasn't a bad thing to have one of Caleb's sisters on her side.

Cassidy surprised her by adding, "I think it's high-time my brother found someone as delightful as you to spend his time with." As an afterthought, she added, "Off the clock."

Smiling at the woman, who was beginning to

seem like she might be a great ally, Willow said, "I couldn't agree more."

With that simple statement, their tentative friendship was sealed.

Even though he couldn't hear their conversation from across the large wooden picnic table they shared, Caleb proved he was not on board with their new alliance by saying in his sister's direction, "It's time for us to take these rugrats home and let Willow get back to her real life."

Willow couldn't imagine a more 'real' life than the one she was glimpsing with Caleb's family in that moment, but she wasn't going to admit that out loud. Nodding briskly, she forced herself to seem ready to leave them as she stood and asked Mickey if he was ready to go.

The kids surprised her by circling her into a group hug, along with their new friend, Buddy. The dog wagged his tail happily, and she knelt down to be closer to their heights.

"Are you coming on the next weekend adventure with us?" Ella's big eyes blinked in her direction.

Willow wanted nothing more than to answer in the affirmative, but she didn't know if Caleb would be amenable to including her again. "We'll see," she responded noncommittally.

When the sweet little girl wrapped her tiny arms around Willow's neck in a tight hug, Willow had to blink back the tears of happiness. She had never encountered such a warm, accepting family. The perpetual ache of loneliness that lingered deep in her stomach erupted with longing to belong with these people.

She realized then that outside of their age gap and Caleb's employment, they were perfect for each other. Those minor problems didn't seem at all insurmountable to her, but when she looked up into Caleb's hooded gaze as Ella hugged her, she realized that he had already closed himself off to the idea of them having a chance as a couple.

Even though she wanted to scream at him that this was exactly what she needed, and that they would be great together, she forced herself to pull back from the little girl. After tweaking Ella's nose, Willow kept her answer deliberately vague when she said, "I would love to come on another adventure with you one of these days."

Ella didn't seem to sense the lack of a firm answer in Willow's response. When she released her arms from around Willow's neck, her face was lit up when she enthused, "I can't wait."

"Me either," Willow answered honestly.

The little girl waved and said, "Bye, Aunt Willow!"

It was then that Willow realized that she didn't stand a chance at resisting the allure of this fabulous family. They had already stolen her heart. Now, she just had to figure out a way to make them love her as much as she already loved them.

*C*aleb couldn't quite believe how seamlessly Willow had fit in with his family. He had assumed she would be aloof with the kids. In reality, she had been the opposite of standoffish. She had effortlessly inserted herself into the mix, and she seemed like she belonged there.

It was all he could do not to reach out to speak to her for the remainder of the weekend. He hated being apart from her, which he knew was a big problem. He prided himself on being a consummate professional, but Willow was turning him into a lovesick sap.

He felt caught because he couldn't trust her safety to anyone else, yet he couldn't seem to control his feelings enough to properly watch over her himself. Her safety, as well as that of her famous dog, was the most important thing in the world to him, but he feared that his ever-growing feelings for her were putting them all at risk.

All day on Sunday, he tried to convince himself that he should admit his feelings to her, quit his job as her protector, and find a suitable replacement. The problem he kept returning to, though, was he didn't feel like he could entrust anyone else with the vital job of keeping Willow and Buddy safe.

The threatening letters she continued to receive were frightening. Caleb believed her life to truly be in danger from this homicidal maniac, and he wanted the best man for the job to be in charge of her care. It sounded conceited, but he knew in his heart that he was the best man to watch over her and keep her safe.

He wouldn't hesitate to give his life for hers. He couldn't say that with certainty about anyone else. Even though it was a requirement of the job, some people didn't have what it took when the time actually came. He was the only one that he knew without a doubt would give his life to save her.

The constant barrage of texts from Cassidy wasn't helping matters. His sister had evidently picked up on the attraction simmering just beneath the surface between him and Willow. She was like a dog with a bone––unwilling to let it go––despite his protestations that she was imagining the connection.

It seemed like Monday morning when Caleb could return to work for Willow would never arrive. He knew he had it bad when he was actually looking forward to Monday.

When he arrived at work to get the lowdown from Mickey, he was livid to find out they had kept the new letter from him when they saw him on Saturday. Even though he had been off-duty, he still wanted to know what was going on with the case.

This new letter was particularly concerning because it had arrived at Willow's house and completely obliterated the pattern that had been previously set. The stalker was stepping up the stakes of the game, so they needed to be on especially high alert.

He couldn't let his guard down for an instant, which made him even more confident in his decision to keep his relationship with Willow strictly professional. Her safety depended on his ability to show restraint where she was concerned... no matter how hard she made it.

The studio was bustling with activity as they geared up for the season finale of Willow's game show. They had done a social media poll on Reel Life to select a winning couple. The audience had spoken, and the very first couple that Buddy had chosen was coming back to get married on a special, live airing of the show. Mandy had been a fan-favorite since the show began airing, so a lot of buzz was building around her wedding and Buddy's first official love match.

This week would be hectic as they prepped for the big show. Caleb was glad that the taping of the show would be going on hiatus for a couple of weeks after the wedding aired. He, Willow, and

Buddy would all be ready for a break after making it through the stress of this busy week.

Mandy and her new fiancé, Joe, were on-set as the preparations were made. They both seemed a little overwhelmed as they looked around with wide eyes, but Caleb was confident that Mandy would make a beautiful bride and that the wedding show would be a huge hit.

This grand finale would make Willow and Buddy's show the hot topic in Redwood Cove. It would seal their show as one that was not to be missed, and it would skyrocket their ratings.

Caleb was glad that Willow and Buddy were seeing so much well-deserved success, but the increased spotlight and fame meant they would be that much harder to keep safe. The more sought-after and popular they were, the more difficult it would be to protect them.

That knowledge made him even more firm in his decision to be Willow's bodyguard--and nothing more. Her safety depended on it.

*T*hat evening when they arrived back at Willow's house, it was raining. It was the first drenching rain they'd had in weeks. Willow had been hoping to go for a walk with her two favorite men, but the rain foiled that plan.

Willow and Caleb stood at the glass patio door that led to her back yard to watch Buddy enjoy playing in the rain. The dog remained frozen for a long moment staring at the gray sky with wonder over the water falling on him. He didn't seem to mind that it was hitting him in the face.

Once he was done pretending to be a statue, his activity level kicked into high gear. He ran and pounced and frolicked in the water as if it was the greatest gift in the world.

Willow couldn't help but smile at her silly pet. She wished she could get so much enjoyment from simple rain. She was more likely to curse it for messing up her hair or getting her expensive leather handbag wet. It had never really dawned on her to appreciate the rain or enjoy playing in it. She usually thought of it more as a necessary evil.

"He's tearing up your yard," Caleb warned her as they watched the dog dig in the mud.

"It can be fixed. He's having fun." Willow responded flippantly, honestly not concerned about the grass.

The look Caleb gave her was filled with a mixture of surprise and warmth. She didn't think she would ever get tired of having him gaze at her like that.

Buddy chose that moment to run onto the porch. Once he slid to a stop, he shook his entire body, sending muddy water flying in every direction. Her pristine white porch was splattered with streaks of filth.

Caleb sucked in a breath as he watched the dog climb up to sit on one of Willow's favorite white rocking chairs. "He's a mess. I guess I better go get some towels to dry him off."

"Thanks." Willow gave Caleb a genuine, grateful smile. There was a time not long ago when she would have been truly upset over the muddy mess on her porch. She realized now, though, that it was just stuff. It was more important to her that Buddy had fun than to keep her belongings in perfect condition.

By the time Caleb returned with several big, fluffy towels, Buddy had jumped down from the rocking chair and was sitting patiently in front of the door, obviously wanting to come inside.

Looking out at him, Caleb said, "Oh, wow… he's a mudball."

"I'll dry him off," Willow offered, holding her

hands out for the towels.

"Nope, I've got it." Caleb smiled down at her. "You stay in here where it's dry and safe."

Willow knew this was way above and beyond the job description of a bodyguard. Mickey would probably have stood with his arms crossed watching her clean off the dog. She couldn't wipe the smile off her face as she peered through the glass while Caleb rubbed Buddy down with the towels.

Once the dog was reasonably clean and dry, Willow opened the door for them. As soon as they walked inside, she reared back. "Eww. What is that horrible acrid odor? It's burning my nostrils."

"That would be wet dog smell." Caleb grinned at her. "Have you not had the displeasure of smelling a wet dog before?"

"Evidently not… it's awful." Willow plugged her nose dramatically. Her voice sounded nasally when she asked nervously, "It goes away, right?"

"It does." Caleb appeased her worries.

The two humans stood there grinning at each other. Breaking the moment, Buddy shook again, sending a spray of cold, wet mud in every direction.

"Ack!" Willow squealed, shielding her face with her arms.

"Sorry about that. I guess he wasn't as dry as I thought." Caleb looked mildly concerned that she might throw a hissy fit.

"It's not your fault," she reassured him, as he knelt down to rub the damp towels over Buddy's fur again.

When Buddy tried to lick the trailing muddy

drops from his face, Caleb leaned back, chuckling good-naturedly. Rubbing one of the towels lightly over Buddy's face, he said, "You silly goon."

Buddy grabbed the yellow towel with his teeth and yanked on his end. Moving a couple of steps toward Willow, the dog shoved his end of the towel towards her abdomen. Unsure what else to do, Willow took ahold of the offering, which Buddy immediately release from his jaw's grip.

Looking down, Willow realized that she and Caleb were both holding ends of the towel. It dawned on her suddenly what her dog was trying to do. "I think Buddy's trying to play matchmaker with us."

Caleb glanced down at the towel before looking back into Willow's eyes. They stood mere inches apart and frozen for a long time. Both of them were breathing heavily as they pondered the monumental decision they needed to make.

Willow was the first to break out of the trance. She absently wiped the back of her hand along her cheek, hoping to remove any errant smudges of mud. "I must look like a mess."

"Far from it." Caleb's voice sounded croaky as he lifted his thumb to her jawline to swipe away a mud streak.

His tender touch sent a shiver of delight along Willow's spine, but she didn't move for fear of breaking the marvelous spell that had been spun between them. They stayed there, suspended as the moment stretched on. Willow longed for him to press his lips down to hers, but she didn't want to be the one to break his carefully held control.

Finally, Caleb looked down at the bright

yellow, muddy towel they were both still holding. Seeming to make a decision, he dropped his end of the towel and lifted that hand to rake his hands through the hair along the nape of Willow's neck.

Stunned by his tingling touch, Willow let the towel fall from her fingers, forgotten.

"Buddy's a professional matchmaker. Who are we to deny his talent?" Caleb's voice was barely above a whisper.

When he tipped his head down, Willow leaned up onto her toes to meet him. His lips brushed lightly across hers, creating a trail of happiness in their wake.

Willow's eyes closed as she pushed up into him, craving more. His lips were soft and pliable, yet demanding. Their kiss was everything she could have dreamed of and more. Her entire body was thrumming with excitement as her mouth tingled with a mysterious sense of being more alive than normal. All of her senses were on high alert as she savored the first meeting of their lips.

After he tore his mouth away from hers, she immediately missed the delightful sensation of his kiss. Her eyes fluttered open and she gazed up at him, feeling utterly mesmerized.

Their arms were still wrapped around each other, which was a good thing, since she felt a little woozy, almost like she was floating on air, from their marvelous first kiss. She found herself aching for another one and hoping that there would be many more just like it to come.

The fact that she was so blown away by a simple connection of their lips made Caleb's words seem even more like a slap in the face.

37

*C*aleb hadn't meant to kiss Willow. In fact, he had promised himself that he wouldn't succumb to that particularly strong desire. He couldn't believe that he had been so weak, but something about her was utterly irresistible.

He knew better than to get involved with a client. He reminded himself that it wasn't in anyone's best interest because it was detrimental to his ability to do a good job, which their lives depended on.

Kissing Willow was glorious--like coming home and sinking into a comfortable couch after a long, hard day at work. It was all he could do to pull his mouth away from hers. His lips felt cold and too alone as soon as they broke apart from hers. He ached to lean down and press them to hers again.

Instead, he forced himself to say, "I'm sorry. That was a mistake. We can't do this."

Then, he turned and left her there alone. He

couldn't be near her now. He didn't have the strength to resist her.

He went to activate the home's alarm system so no one could breach the perimeter of the house, then he went to his room to hide and brood. If he stayed around Willow right now, he would end up kissing her again. He needed to be alone to renew his willpower and remind himself why he was here.

His job was to keep Willow and Buddy safe. That was all that mattered. Kissing her was a distraction from that goal, so he wouldn't allow it to happen again… He couldn't.

After a cold shower, during which he berated himself for being weak, Caleb paced his room. Anger filled him over the stalker who was threatening Willow and Buddy's safety. That maniac was the one Caleb needed to focus on. He would have to put any romantic feelings that were developing for Willow out of his mind until that threat was eliminated.

"All the more reason to catch him." Caleb said through gritted teeth as he stalked to the far side of his room.

Turning, and walking back, he forced all thoughts of Willow out of his mind. Any chance he might have with her would have to wait until the threat on her life was eliminated and his job was complete. Until then, he wasn't even going to think of Willow as being female.

He couldn't help but chuckle at the preposterous nature of that as he turned on his heel and went back the direction he'd come from. Willow was the most desirable woman he had ever encountered. "Easier said than done," he mumbled in frustration to the empty room.

Keeping his promise to himself, Caleb was all business the next morning. He anticipated that there would be a Tuesday letter from the stalker, and he wanted all cylinders to be firing at full-speed when he inspected it.

Even though the nutcase had stepped up his efforts by adding in a weekend threat, Caleb was confident that he would still follow his previously set pattern and send one on his 'normal' day.

Sure enough, after the mail delivery, one of the producers of *Matched*, asked Willow and Caleb to come up to the big conference room for a meeting. Caleb knew without being told that another letter had arrived, but the drawn look on the producer's face indicated that this one was somehow worse.

Caleb's stomach soured with dread as they followed the man out of the studio. When the producer pushed the button for the elevator, Willow and Caleb hung back, reminding the man that Buddy didn't like riding it. By silent agreement the trio took the stairs.

Caleb was impressed that Willow could now climb flight after flight, without seeming to get winded. Just weeks ago, she had been panting for breath when they reached the top floor. It was such a loving gesture for her to hoof it, rather than forcing her dog to do something he feared. Before he met her, Caleb never would have thought Willow would do something so selfless. Now that he knew her, he realized it was classic Willow. She would do anything for those she loved. Buddy was a lucky dog to have chosen her as his pet parent.

Caleb's musings screeched to a halt when they crossed the threshold into the main conference room. The usual people that met every week to discuss the latest letter were here––several studio executives, producers, production assistants, and a representative from the police force. Today, though, two plain-clothes detectives had been added to the mix.

Caleb hoped the additions meant that the police department wanted to step-up their efforts to catch this lunatic. He feared, though, that the detectives were here because of a heightened threat level.

His concerns were proved to be correct, when one of the detectives stepped forward and cleared his throat. He looked directly at Willow as he spoke. "Ms. Winks, the studio received a very concerning letter today."

"It's Tuesday," Willow quipped, obviously not sensing that this letter was somehow worse than the others.

"Maybe you better have a look at it." The detective slid the note across the slick table in her direction.

Caleb leaned over to see it. He instantly recognized the intricately cut letters. It was obviously from the same person as the others had been, but this one was chillingly different. Rather than being a generic threat, it specified exactly when and where the madman planned to attack.

After quickly scanning to get the gist of the letter, Caleb read it slowly and carefully.

. . .

You think you've found a perfect match.
   But it's you I'm going to catch.
   Your big wedding show
   Is going to be a huge fiasco.
   Keep a close eye on Willow Winks
   Because as soon as she blinks
   I'll pull out my gun
   And her life will be done.

"He's planning to attack during the wedding ceremony on the show's finale." Caleb said the words aloud as he processed the meaning of this latest threat.

Even though everyone else had already read the letter, they nodded solemnly in agreement as Caleb and Willow absorbed what this meant.

Caleb didn't have to think about it long before making a decision. "The show has to be cancelled."

"What?!? Absolutely not." The suit at the head of the table blustered.

Caleb glared at him and calmly stated the facts. "Willow and Buddy's safety is the only thing that matters. Now that we know his plans, we can eliminate the threat to them by cancelling the show."

The executive's face instantly flushed a vivid reddish-purple color. "We can't cancel it. Do you know how much promotion and advertising has gone into this finale? It's not an option."

Fury iced Caleb's veins as he realized the studio executives were more worried about money and profit than their stars' safety. "It's not an option to film it when we know Willow and Buddy will be in danger. Besides, do you really think the bride and groom want to take the chance of their wedding ceremony becoming a shooting range?"

"We'll step-up security. We will turn this place into Fort Knox." The head honcho promised.

"This person is crazy. He doesn't care about his own safety, and he'll do anything to get to Willow and Buddy. We can't take that kind of risk with their lives." Caleb couldn't believe he had to point this out as he tried to talk some sense into them.

He turned towards the detectives, hoping to get some support on his assertion that it was crazy to even think about filming the show when they knew Willow and Buddy's lives would be in danger.

The detective in the cheap blue suit nodded, and for a moment Caleb thought he was going to back him up. Instead, he said, "This might be our best chance to catch this maniac and put an end to these threats. We know he'll be nearby during filming, so we can use an extensive team to find and capture him."

"So, you want to use Willow as bait?" Caleb practically spat the words out.

"We'll keep her safe." The other detective spoke for the first time.

Caleb felt like jumping out of his seat to strangle him. Since that wasn't an option, he accused, "You can't know that."

"We'll do everything we can to keep her safe."

Blue suit toned down the other detective's bold promise.

"That's not enough." Caleb spoke through tightly-gritted teeth. He wasn't willing to risk Willow or Buddy's safety in this manner.

The man at the head of the table leaned forward. "We can't just *not* do the show's finale. There is too much riding on it."

"Why not? There are more important things than money." When Caleb saw the crestfallen expression on Willow's face, he felt like punching the studio executive in the jaw.

It wasn't until she spoke that he realized her downcast expression wasn't due to the man's heartless attitude. It was actually one of determination. Her voice sounded calm and clear when she said firmly, "We're not cancelling the show."

Quickly realizing that Willow had dug her feet in and wasn't going to budge on this matter, Caleb said, "Then we need to reschedule it. We can move the filming to a secret date and location. Only those who absolutely must know will be informed of the revised details."

Turning her clear blue gaze to him, Willow lifted her chin and said, "No."

Caleb started to object, but something about the fiery, determined look in her eyes made him hold back.

When Willow spoke, it was with a finality that didn't permit any questioning of her authority. "This is Mandy and Joe's wedding, and we aren't going to ruin it by changing the venue or date."

When Caleb opened his mouth, her firm head shake left no room for objection.

"The bride and groom have guests flying in from all over the country. We will create the perfect special day for them."

Unable to hold back any longer, Caleb said, "With bullets flying past their heads."

"You'll keep us safe." Willow's voice held more confidence in his abilities than he felt. Looking to the detectives for confirmation, she said, "You'll all make sure everyone is kept safe."

The blue-suited detective's brisk nod must have been enough to ease her concerns because she steeled her resolve, lifted her chin, and said, "The show must go on."

38

*W*illow's proclamation set the room in motion. She wished she felt as confident as she had sounded that everything would be fine with the show's finale.

She refused to put her life on halt for the maniac that was threatening her. Besides, Mandy would be devastated if they had to postpone her nuptials. The wedding had been meticulously planned by the bride––with the help of the show's producers. Changing the timing or venue would throw a wrench into those plans. This was Mandy's big day, and Willow refused to risk any part of it.

The fact that it was the grand finale to the first season of Willow's new show was secondary to the wedding. There was once a time when she would have considered her show's success the most important thing in the world. Spending time with Buddy and Caleb had helped her see that her show was actually fairly far down on her priority list.

Not wanting to make the final decision without at least consulting the bride and groom, Willow asked that Mandy and Joe be sent up to the conference room. Some of the big wigs cleared out, but the executive producers, detectives, Willow, Buddy, and Caleb stayed.

Once the wide-eyed bride was ushered into the room, Willow invited her to sit down. Her fiancé stood nervously behind her chair.

Willow took a deep, calming breath. "There's no easy way to say this," she warned them as she slid the latest letter across the table towards them. "There is a lunatic who has been threatening Buddy and me for several months. He has recently stepped-up his efforts and is now saying he will attack us at your wedding."

Mandy gasped and lifted a hand to cover her mouth. Her groom-to-be immediately moved to put his hand on her shoulder to comfort her, impressing Willow immensely. She smiled, despite the grim circumstances, and thought to herself that Buddy might just know what he was doing when it came to matchmaking.

The room was silent for a long moment as everyone gave the engaged couple time to process the threat that hung over their big day. Mandy looked up at Willow. Her gorgeous green eyes were blinking back tears when she said, "We need to move the wedding. We can't jeopardize your safety."

Caleb breathed a deep, audible sigh of relief that at least someone was being logical about all of this. Looking up towards the ceiling, he said in a voice barely above a whisper, "Thank you."

"Now, hold on." Willow gave the young woman a kind smile. "I appreciate you being willing to modify your plans, but it isn't necessary."

"Yes, it is," Caleb interjected.

Holding up her hand to stop him from speaking, Willow continued. "We have all discussed it, and no one wants to let one crazy person ruin your big day." Pointing to the detectives still hovering in the corner of the room, she added, "These kind gentleman have agreed to put together a top-of-the-line security detail to keep everyone safe. My personal bodyguard will be there, too." She waved her hand in Caleb's direction.

Mandy's expression was filled with uncertainty, so Willow looked at the show's producers for confirmation as she said, "I'm sure we can also hire bodyguards to be by your sides for the duration as well."

One of the executive producers nodded his approval for the extra expense.

Willow reached out to place her hand on Mandy's in a comforting gesture. "We know these aren't ideal circumstances, so if you want to move the wedding to a secret location or date, we will. But we are prepared to go forward with the ceremony as planned, if you are."

Mandy seemed uncertain about what to say. She shook her head. "We can't have you and Buddy risking your lives just so that we get our dream wedding. It's not worth it."

Even though her words were saying that she wanted to change their planned wedding, the tears streaming uncontrollably down her cheeks told another story. Willow appreciated the bride-to-be's kindheartedness and bravery. She wanted to do anything in her power to make sure this lovely young woman had the perfect wedding she deserved.

"We won't be at any more risk than we are at any other time." Willow assured her. "This lunatic has been threatening us for months. Besides, security will be heightened to the point that no one will be able to get near us. Right?"

She looked towards the detectives in the corner for back-up because she could feel the fear and annoyance emanating in waves from Caleb's direction.

"That's right." Blue suit confirmed, adding a brisk nod.

Caleb's chair shot back from the table as he stood. Practically shouting, he yelled, "He won't have to get near you if he's using a long-range rifle."

The room sat in stunned silence for a long moment as they pondered his harsh, sobering words.

Some mysterious stubborn streak made Willow unable to back down. She refused to give in and let a madman control her life. Shoving her own chair back and standing to square off with Caleb she said, "Then I guess we'll have to secure the surrounding areas. You were in the Secret Service--I'm sure you can figure it out."

With that, Willow stormed out of the room, hoping that she hadn't just signed her own--or anyone else's--death sentence.

39

The last thing Caleb wanted to do was follow Willow out of that meeting room, but he didn't have any other choice. He would have much rather gone off on his own to find something to punch--hard and repeatedly.

He couldn't believe Willow had chosen this crisis moment to showcase her stubborn diva streak. Jeopardizing her safety was the one thing he couldn't allow, yet that was exactly what she was insisting on--all for a stupid wedding. It didn't make sense, but he couldn't seem to make her see that.

She had made her decision, and she wasn't willing to budge an inch. She trusted him to keep them safe, but he didn't like the odds that were stacked against him. Caleb had the feeling that this lunatic would do whatever it took to get to his targets. Caleb was willing to do anything to make sure that didn't happen, but he feared the maniac might find a way through his defenses.

He would never be able to forgive himself if someone was hurt on his watch. That's why he knew he wouldn't hesitate to jump in front of a bullet for his charges––because his life would be over, even if he didn't.

Knowing the when and where of a planned attack didn't make it any easier, though. If anything, it made it harder because he would be so fearful of missing something.

Just the thought of someone shooting at Willow and Buddy made his blood chill. During the time he had been watching over them, they had become so much more to him than simple charges that he worked to protect. The famous duo had somehow weaseled their way deep into his heart––despite his intentions to the contrary.

He rounded on Willow as soon as the door slammed behind them in her dressing room. His instinct was to yell at her to try to make her see reason, but he knew that wouldn't get him far with the stubborn woman. Instead, he allowed his vulnerability to show. "Please don't do this."

Her expression immediately softened. She had obviously been expecting anger from him. She huffed out a breath, before saying, "I have to."

"You don't." He reminded fervently. "We can find another way to make Mandy's wedding everything she hopes for. A way that won't risk anyone's life."

"If we do that, he wins." Willow's blue eyes were pleading with Caleb to understand where she was coming from.

"No." Caleb shook his head stubbornly. "As long as you stay safe, we win."

"I trust you to keep me safe." Her eyes were filled with an unwavering faith that he didn't deserve.

"Don't." He warned her. When he saw the crestfallen look darken her beautiful eyes, he took both of her hands within his own before clarifying. "I will do anything in my power to keep you safe... always."

The relieved expression on her face was undeniable. Not wanting her to become too confident, he added, "I'm just worried that your stalker will find a way through our best defenses. Since we know when and where he's planning to strike, I can't, in good conscience, send you out there to face that danger. It would be reckless and playing right into his hand."

Willow shook her head. "He expects us to give in. He wants to make us bend to his will, or he wouldn't have told us when and where to expect his attack. We need to face it and not back down."

Caleb ran his hands through his hair as he stalked across the room. He wondered if his strong feelings for Willow were affecting his judgment. Normally, he was supremely confident in his job skills, and he never backed down from a challenge. This was too much, though. The mere thought of putting Willow and Buddy in danger made him feel nauseous.

It would be fantastic to catch this nut and put an end to the constant threat hanging over their lives, but the risk was too great. He couldn't abide by it, unless there was an absolute guarantee of Willow and Buddy's safety, and that wasn't possible.

His eyes lit up with an idea and he whirled around to face Willow. "We know that security will be too tight for him to get into the studio, so he will be attempting to strike from a distance."

Willow nodded. Curiosity over where he was going with this was visible on her face.

"What if we use a body double for you? Someone from the police force, who is trained…"

"Absolutely not." Willow interrupted him, seeming unwilling to even consider his idea.

"But we could find someone that…" Caleb started, but stopped when Willow held her palm up. He huffed in frustration that she wasn't even willing to listen to his argument.

"I can't put anyone else in danger like that. It's bad enough that you'll be out there with me. This is my problem, not anyone else's."

Willow's concern for everyone else's safety over her own made Caleb want to protect her even more. "I'm paid to take care of you. It's my job." He reminded her gently.

Tears welled in her lower lids when she whispered under her breath, "I would never forgive myself if something happened to you, while you're watching over me."

Caleb knew exactly how she felt because his life would be worthless if something happened to Willow––whether he was on bodyguard duty with her or not. Instead of voicing that alarming reality, he settled for saying, "Same."

The look she gave him was filled with warmth and a spark of something more. When she wrapped her arms around his neck to give him a hug, Caleb hoped that meant she was growing to care about him––even if it was a tiny fraction of his feelings for her.

When Willow pulled back she looked up into his eyes and said, "We can't back down from this threat. It's been hanging over our heads for too long. I need this to be over."

Caleb hated it that he hadn't considered the strain that Willow must be under with a constant threat weighing heavily on her mind. It was too much stress to endure on a long-term basis.

As much as Caleb hated to put her in any danger, he knew that the longer this lingered on, the man threatening them would only become braver and more radical. The madman had already escalated things to an unprecedented level. If they didn't catch him and put a stop to it, he would likely amp things up even further. It wasn't like he was going to change his mind at this point and go away. He had taken it too far to back down now.

Caleb savored the awe-filled look Willow was giving him. Silently praying that he could live up to her faith in him, he said, "Okay... If you insist, the show will go on as planned."

*E*ven though Willow had insisted that they move forward with the wedding show season finale as planned, now that it was here, she regretted her vehemence. She wanted the threat that had been hanging over her head for so long to be lifted, but she didn't want anyone to be hurt in the process.

If someone was injured during the taping of this finale, she would never forgive herself. *Why had she been such a stubborn diva about this? Why hadn't she listened to Caleb?* These thoughts were on constant replay in her mind as her makeup artist, Lacy, swiped a fluffy blush brush across her face… again.

"You are as white as a sheet today. Even my darkest mauve shade of 'Let's Get Cheeky' isn't improving your pallor." Lacy commented as she absently used a sponge to blend the colors together.

"Must be wedding day jitters," Willow quipped,

trying to make light of the ominous threat hanging over her head.

Evidently deciding to play along with her avoidance technique, Lacy stated the obvious. "Well, it's not *your* wedding."

Enjoying thinking about something other than the prospect of bullets flying past their heads today, Willow said, "It's the first one I've officiated, though. My brand-new ordainment certificate from the internet makes it legitimate."

Lacy chuckled as she glanced at the printed certificate proudly displayed on Willow's mirror. "You can do anything online nowadays, huh?" At Willow's nod, Lacy asked, "Have you ever joined any of the online dating sites?"

"No, I think I'd prefer to meet someone the old fashioned way," Willow told her, thinking of how she'd met Caleb. He would be perfect if he was a few years older, and if he didn't work for her.

"My friend, Margot, met her husband through one of those sites," Lacy revealed.

Willow smiled as she looked at Lacy in the mirror's reflection and encouraged the woman to go on. She knew from years of experience with her that the chatterbox would happily carry the conversation with only an encouraging head nod or one-word question here and there required from Willow. Sometimes Lacy's nonstop babbling bothered Willow, but today she was glad for the distraction.

When Lacy proclaimed her hair and makeup to be finished, Willow's stomach churned uncomfortably. She couldn't imagine how nervous poor Mandy must be, with both wedding day jitters and the knowledge of a madman out to get them.

It was tempting to hide out in her dressing room, but she knew she needed to face this directly or the threat would continue to hang in a dark cloud over her. She needed a break from the fear that had been her constant companion for the last few months, and today was the day to make it happen. She could feel the nervous tension of momentous changes practically crackling in the air. Something big was about to happen—in addition to Mandy's wedding and her show's season finale. Things were about to come to a head with the person who had been threatening her. She just prayed that no one would be hurt in the process.

If Willow was pale, Caleb was practically ghost-like. He was waiting right outside her dressing room door, and his frightened, grayish pallor did nothing to ease her concerns.

He was normally her rock, but today, it was obvious that the stress of having a maniac after them was weighing heavily on his mind.

She wished there was something she could do to ease his worries, but they were valid and real. He had every right to be concerned. They all did.

After licking her dry lips and clearing her throat, she held her elbow out towards Caleb and said, "Shall we?" Despite her best intentions to seem calm, her voice came out sounding croaky and uncertain.

Caleb looked at her for a long moment. She wondered if he was about to insist that they leave and reschedule the taping. A small part of her wished that he would. Instead, he gave her a slight head nod and accepted her offered elbow by looping his arm through it.

Just the simple touch of their interlocked arms was soothing to Willow. This was easily the most frightening, stressful day of her life. She wouldn't want to face it with anyone other than Caleb by her side.

Reminding Willow that he was her other rock, Buddy leaned gently onto her other leg. She absently rested a hand on the soft fur of his head. The intuitive dog seemed to sense that she needed extra comfort today, and his adoring gaze up at her provided it.

Flanked by her two favorite males, Willow made her way to the stairs to head down to the studio. The network hadn't been stingy with security for the big day. Two armed bodyguards led the way down the stairs, and another two followed behind them. If anything went wrong today, it wouldn't be due to a lack of precautions.

The in-studio audience had been limited to Mandy and Joe's invited wedding guests. Each person who wished to attend was being patted down and sent through a metal detector. The security at this wedding was more stringent than most airports.

Willow waited out of sight on the sidelines of the stage as the guests filed slowly in and took their seats. The wedding rehearsal had gone perfectly, which made her nervous that today might be a complete fiasco.

Smiling to herself, she realized that it didn't

matter if she flubbed every word of the ceremony or tripped and knocked over the happy couple, as long as no one was shot at. It was hard to believe that the low bar of everyone staying alive was her main concern on the biggest day of her career.

The nervous energy was practically zinging around the studio. Much of it was emanating from the side of her body where Caleb was standing, methodically scanning the room. Buddy was practically dancing by her other side as his feet clacked nervously on the slick floors. He must have picked up on the high anxiety in the room because he seemed to sense that today was special.

Jerry, her hype-man was subdued today as he spoke to the crowd once everyone was seated. He normally had them clapping, laughing, and desperate to see Willow and Buddy. Today, he calmly announced that the wedding ceremony would begin soon and gave them a few instructions for the show's taping, like ignoring the cameras and remaining quiet during the vows.

Once he was finished, it was time for Willow and Buddy to take the stage. Today's crowd was different because many of them were from out of town. They didn't recognize her because her show only aired locally in the Redwood Cove area.

Willow took a deep breath and prepared to walk out to greet the crowd. Just as she took her first step, Caleb grabbed her arm to hold her back. Since her nerves were already on high-alert, she feared that he had seen a gun or some other threat that she had missed.

She froze in place and grabbed his hand, squeezing it within hers. She knew that he would need his hand to properly do his job, but she couldn't seem to let him go.

He returned her tight grip as if he needed to hold onto her, too. When she finally turned to look at his face, what she saw there was an expression that perfectly mirrored her own feelings: fear, almost to the point of panic, and... love.

"Willow, I..." Caleb's face was drawn as his warm gaze enveloped her.

That look of pure love gave her the confidence she needed to go on. Beaming up at him, she said, "I know... me too."

With that, she let go of her death grip on his hand and walked out on stage.

*M*andy was a beautiful bride. The bouquet of pale pink peonies shook nervously as she walked down the aisle towards her groom, but her wide smile never wavered.

Joe beamed at her with a look of unadulterated love that perfectly mimicked the gaze Caleb had just bestowed on Willow as they stood beside the stage.

Caleb stood just out of the range of the camera, quietly scanning the room and watching every move. The rest of the security detail was scattered about, but it was Caleb's presence that gave Willow the confidence to go on.

Despite her nerves, Willow's voice sounded calm and clear as she officiated the ceremony. Buddy provided a bit of comedic relief when he got tired of standing and plopped down on Willow's feet with a great huff of exasperation.

The happy couple had written their own vows.

There wasn't a dry eye left in the room, except those of the security team, when Joe proclaimed his undying love for Mandy and thanked Buddy for choosing him. It was a sweet, heartfelt speech that made Willow's heart feel like it might burst with pride over her intuitive dog.

Once the rings were exchanged, Willow breathed a sigh of relief. Perhaps the extra security had scared off the madman, or maybe he changed his mind. No matter the reasoning, the wedding ceremony was nearly over, and nothing had gone wrong.

With a sigh of relief and a wide, happy smile, Willow said proudly, "I now pronounce you husband and wife. You may kiss the…"

In that moment, before she could finish her sentence, craziness ensued. She heard Caleb shout, "The air duct!" as he lunged in her direction. All eyes turned to look at where he had pointed as he leaped. Several security officers whirled around, removing guns from their jackets.

The shots rang out, echoing loudly around the studio. People screamed and dove for cover. Joe hurled his body over his surprised bride. Willow watched in horror as the entire scene seemed to play out in slow motion before her.

She barely had time to register what was happening as she fell to the ground. Her hip, shoulder, and head slammed into the floor with frightening sounding cracks. The pain immediately spread through her as she tried to figure out if one of the fired bullets had hit her.

It wasn't until she felt the dead weight on her that she realized that Caleb was on top of her.

Buddy sniffed and whined as he nudged at the two of them.

Chaos prevailed around them as people screamed, ran, and sobbed. Willow barely comprehended any of it as she looked at the spreading pool of bright red blood between them and tried to determine if it was she or Caleb who had been shot.

"*C*aleb? Caleb!" She shouted, shaking him lightly and desperate for a response. When none came, numbness overtook her body.

She didn't know if she had been shot, too, and she didn't care. All that mattered was that Caleb had been hurt trying to protect her, and she needed to get him medical attention.

It dawned on her for a brief moment that the shooter might not have been subdued, but her own safety was not as important as making sure Caleb received treatment for his gunshot wound. She gently rolled him off her, placing her own body between him and the direction the shots had come from. Some primal instinct deep within her had to make sure he wasn't injured any further.

When she saw the large, growing red circle on his shirt, she gasped. Her own dress was also covered in blood, but she feared it was Caleb's.

Desperate to stop his bleeding, she yanked off her colorful silk scarf and pressed it to the area as her eyes frantically searched the chaotic studio for help. People were running in all directions, panicked and uncertain where to hide.

She made eye contact with Joe as he shielded his bride's body with his own. "Call 9-1-1," Willow ordered him, hoping that he had his phone on him, since she had left hers in her dressing room for the taping.

Joe nodded his understanding and groped in his suit pocket for his phone. Willow kept pressure on Caleb's chest and talked to him--uncertain what else to do to revive him. Buddy angled his body alongside Caleb's and whined as he licked the unconscious man's hand.

The gunshots had stopped, but the panicked hysteria continued as people scrambled for safety. When she finally heard sirens in the distance, Willow sobbed with relief.

She leaned down and was thankful when she heard Caleb's ragged breathing. "Please hold on. Help is on its way." She promised him, whispering near his ear.

When the uniformed EMTs found them, one of them said, "Ms. Winks, you're covered in blood. Have you been shot?"

"I don't think so. It's Caleb." She nodded towards where she was holding the blood-soaked scarf. "He's been shot in the chest. Please help him," she pleaded.

"We'll do our best," the other man promised as they leaned down to rip open Caleb's shirt to do an assessment of his injury. Before long they had him strapped on a stretcher and were rushing him out to an ambulance.

Willow ran after them, but was stopped by the CEO of the studio. "Willow, are you okay?" He asked her with his eyes open wide in fright.

"I'm fine, but Caleb has been injured." She moved quickly past him and ran outside, but Caleb's ambulance was already wheeling away with the siren blaring.

Unwilling to wait for Nico and her normal car service, Willow jumped into the passenger seat of the limo that was waiting at the sidewalk for the bride and groom's big exit.

"Follow that ambulance," she ordered the surprised driver as Buddy leaped over her to sit in the middle.

"No dogs," the driver started to object, but Willow indicated her blood-soaked dress with her hand, effectively stopping him in his tracks.

"It's not open for discussion… Ambulance," she said firmly as she pointed at the vehicle, leaving him no room to question her direction.

Seeming to suddenly comprehend the urgency, the driver squealed the tires as he took off in hot pursuit of Caleb's ambulance.

The car was still rolling to a stop in front of Gold Coast General Hospital's emergency room when Willow jumped out with Buddy hot on her heels. As soon as they ran inside, a woman in scrubs tried to stop them. "No dogs are allowed in the hospital, unless they are service animals."

Willow turned to tell her that Buddy was coming with her and it wasn't up for discussion when recognition dawned on the woman's face. "Willow? Buddy? Oh-my-gosh… I can't believe it's really you." When her gaze traveled down to

Willow's bloody dress, she gasped, "Are you okay?"

"Yes, but my bodyguard has been hurt. I need to find him... Caleb McCreery." Her eyes silently pleaded with the other woman for help.

Turning all business, the nurse said, "Come with me. We'll find him."

Willow wasn't normally one to take advantage of the special star-treatment her celebrity status provided her, but when it came to Caleb's care or finding out about his condition, she would use any means available.

The nurse found a freestanding computer station and tapped her fingernails quickly on the keyboard. Once she had the information she was looking for, she turned to Willow and said, "Follow me."

Willow and Buddy stayed right behind the quick-moving nurse. Since they looked like they were on a mission, no one else stopped to question Buddy's right to be there. Once they approached the curtained area and Willow peeked in, it was obvious that they had found Caleb.

Medical professionals were scurrying around as they assessed the damage to his body. She knew that she had no legal right to be standing there watching as they worked on him, but it was where she belonged.

Quick as a wink, they had him prepped for surgery, and his gurney was whisked down the hallway towards the elevator. Willow didn't dare stop any of the doctors or nurses for fear that every second counted with getting Caleb into surgery to remove the bullet lodged in his chest.

One person remained in the area tapping an electronic tablet, likely recording the events that had transpired for Caleb's medical chart. Willow assumed the oversized man was some type of orderly. She was unable to keep the desperation out of her voice when she asked, "Is Caleb going to be okay?"

The large man in putrid green scrubs looked startled to see her and uncertain if he should respond. They stared at each other in silence for a long moment.

"Please," Willow tried. "The man who was just in here... He's my bodyguard, and he was injured saving me."

When the man started to shake his head, Willow feared that he wasn't going to give her any information about Caleb's condition. Frantic for any news, she quickly added, "And I love him."

It was the first time she had said the actual words out loud. The orderly's dark, wary gaze softened immediately at her confession. Evidently opting to bend the rules, he said somberly, "It doesn't look good." Willow gasped with fright, but forced herself to remain quiet to hear the rest of what this man had to say. "Fortunately, the bullet missed his heart, but it still did a lot of damage and he lost a lot of blood."

Willow nodded her quiet acceptance, hoping he would give her more information. She needed a wisp of hope to hold on to while she waited for news from Caleb's surgery.

Evidently understanding her silent plea, the man went on. "They'll do everything they can to help him survive the surgery, but he suffered a major trauma."

Willow's face must have looked as crestfallen as she felt at this news because he softened his tone when he said, "I'm sorry that I can't give you better news, but you need to prepare yourself that he most likely won't make it out of surgery alive."

A sob escaped Willow's throat as she pondered for the first time a world without Caleb in it. Even though she knew if he survived, it was likely that he would move on and find someone his own age to spend his life with, she couldn't fathom him not being around.

There was no denying the spark of hope that they might actually end up together, but even if they didn't make a go of it as a couple, she wanted him to live a long, happy life. He was far too young and had too much potential to have it snuffed out before he had a chance to truly start living.

The orderly had the uncomfortable look that men usually adopt when women cry. He swiped his beefy hand along the back of his neck before saying, "Look, miracles happen every day."

It wasn't much to hold onto, but it was all she had. She appreciated his honesty and the tiny bit of hope that he had given her. She was going to clutch onto it and never let it go. Caleb was going to pull out of this and make a full recovery, even if it took a miracle. If anyone deserved divine intervention at a time like this, it was generous, brave Caleb.

That tiny spark of hope was just beginning to fully register in Willow's heart when the cavalry arrived. The orderly took the opportunity to make a quick exit as a crowd from the studio circled Willow and rapid-fired questions in her direction.

Everyone looked frazzled as Willow did her best to catch everyone up on Caleb's condition. She sagged with relief when she found out that no one else had been hurt, other that some minor scrapes and bruises from diving for cover from the spray of bullets whizzing past them.

Dash Diamond and his wife, Grace, put supportive arms around Willow as the entire group moved to the waiting room area. Willow let herself sink into the embrace of her kind friends before suddenly sitting upright.

"We have to notify Caleb's family!" Her eyes were wide open and burning as she thought about Caleb's single mother, sisters, and boisterous nieces and nephews getting the news of his injury.

"I'll take care of it." The production assistant had already pulled out her cell phone to track down a phone number for the family.

Once their large group was situated in the emergency room's waiting area, Willow asked if they had caught the shooter. No one seemed to know what had happened, since they had rushed to get here to check on Caleb's condition.

"I'm sure the police will update us as soon as things settle down," the studio's CEO assured the group.

When Willow noticed Mandy and Joe sitting quietly to the side with their families, she said earnestly to them, "I'm so sorry your wedding was ruined."

"It's not your fault," Mandy's eyes were wide with sincerity.

Joe added, "We're sorry this happened to you, and we hope your bodyguard is going to be okay."

"Me too," Willow whispered quietly.

Somber silence overtook the room. Even Buddy seemed to be aware of the seriousness of the situation as he rested calmly near Willow's feet. There seemed to be nothing to do now, but wait.

43

*C*aleb's family ran frantically into the hospital as a large group. They were obviously distraught as they all spoke at once, requesting information on Caleb's condition. Willow told them what she knew, but it wasn't nearly enough. His mother and sisters looked gray with worry as they found seats in the crowded waiting area.

When the police finally arrived at the hospital to give them an update, Willow squeezed Grace's hand tightly within her own. She hoped they had caught the lunatic who had shot Caleb and that they would lock him away for a very long time.

One of the detectives that Willow recognized from the meeting where they read the weekend threat letter crouched down in front of her. He spoke in a deep, calm voice. "The suspect has been apprehended."

A collective sigh of relief emitted from the group. Willow hadn't allowed herself to think about the possibility of him getting away and coming to finish his quest to kill her and Buddy, but now that she knew he had been captured, relief overwhelmed her.

"Do you know who he is and why he targeted Willow?" Dash asked.

"Yes on both counts," the detective answered before explaining. "The suspect appeared on your first show. Neither Mandy, nor Buddy, picked him as the winning bachelor, and he's extremely bitter about it."

Mandy gulped in a breath, squeezed her eyes shut, and covered her mouth with her hand. Joe pulled her into a hug, and she sobbed quietly into his shoulder.

Willow tried to picture the third bachelor from their very first show. He hadn't seemed deranged or frightening––even after he wasn't chosen. She couldn't believe he had gone so far off the deep end and blamed her and her innocent dog for the fact that he wasn't selected as the winning bachelor.

Mandy's voice sounded squeaky when she said, "This is all my fault."

Several members of the group said, "No," in unison, but it was Willow who comforted the distraught bride. "This is absolutely not your fault, or anyone else's in this room," she paused to make eye contact with each person in the group to enunciate her point. "The only one to blame is the homicidal maniac, who went crazy because he lost on a game show."

Turning to address Mandy directly again, Willow said, "I'm glad you didn't pick him.

Imagine how he would have reacted when you realized he was crazy and dumped him."

It wasn't funny, but it broke the ice enough that Mandy smiled through her tears at the thought. A couple of people chuckled lightly.

The detective stood back up and addressed the entire group. "We have a solid case against the shooter. He won't be seeing daylight for a very, very long time."

A few handclaps and half-hearted woo-hoos sounded, but for the most part, they were all too worried about Caleb to celebrate the capture of the dangerous criminal.

Once the detectives and uniformed police officers left, the room once again silenced. It seemed like an eternity as they waited for any news of Caleb's condition.

Willow glanced over and noticed Mandy's rumpled wedding dress as she rested on her groom's chest. Willow had been so caught up in the tragic events and her worry over Caleb that she had forgotten this was the biggest day of their young lives.

Knowing that they were too polite to leave on their own, Willow said, "You two need to go get some rest, so you can enjoy your honeymoon trip to Hawaii the show is sending you on tomorrow."

Glancing at the time on his phone, Dash realized it was after midnight and corrected her. "Make that today."

Willow couldn't believe so much time had passed.

It was Mandy that answered, but Joe nodded

his agreement, when she said, "We're not going anywhere until we hear how Caleb is doing."

The stubborn tilt of her chin made it obvious that the young woman wasn't going to budge on this, so Willow nodded her head at them. She hated it that they felt any responsibility for what had happened, but she understood their need to see this through to the end.

Turning to address the larger group from the studio, Willow said, "You all can go home. We will update you as soon as we have any news on Caleb."

No one moved an inch. They were all here for the long haul.

"We're not going anywhere," Grace assured her.

Willow wondered briefly who was watching Dash and Grace's kids, but she remembered then that they had a neighbor who was their family-by-choice. Deciding she was sure they had it covered and thankful for their calming presence, Willow leaned on Grace's shoulder and let the woman's soothing grip on her hand give her strength.

After many hours, the team of weary surgeons emerged through the swinging double doors into the waiting area. Caleb's family and Willow ran anxiously towards them. The tiny woman standing in front of them removed her 49ers-themed surgeon's cap and looked at Willow as she spoke. "It was touch-and-go for a long time in there. We almost lost him twice on the table."

Caleb's mother looked like she might pass out. Cassidy wrapped her arm around her mom, keeping her upright. Willow covered her own mouth with her palm as the tears blazed trails down her cheeks. She forced herself to remain quiet, so the surgeon would continue with her update on Caleb's condition.

"But he's very strong, and he pulled through the surgery. We were able to get the bullet out, but he's still at risk for internal bleeding. We'll need to monitor him closely for the next few days. If he makes it, he'll be in a lot of pain, but I expect he will make a full recovery."

Cassidy asked, "Can we see him?"

"In the morning," the doctor promised before turning to go back through the double doors.

Choosing not to focus on the 'if he makes it' wording, Willow replayed the doctor's final words over and over in her mind after the team of doctors left. 'He will make a full recovery' was her new mantra.

After they found out that Caleb made it through surgery, the studio staff made Willow promise to call with any news on Caleb's condition before they left.

Mandy and Joe looked like they intended to stay through the night, until Willow convinced them it was silly. After many hugs and promises to call the minute she heard anything further about Caleb, she sent the kindhearted newlyweds on their way.

Soon, it was just Caleb's family, Willow, Dash, and Grace left in the waiting room, along with various strangers.

Willow was grateful that it was Saturday, so Dash wouldn't be expected to try to do a show so soon after the attack. Turning to look at Dash and

Grace, Willow said, "Don't you guys need to get home to your kids?"

"We're not going anywhere," Grace assured her.

Even though she would have understood if they needed to leave, Willow was relieved that they were insisting on staying with her. Cassidy and the children were the only members of Caleb's family that she had met prior to today, and she would have felt like an intruder if she had been left here alone with them.

The kids were remarkably calm as they stretched out across their mothers' laps and dozed off. Everyone finally fell asleep, except for Willow and Caleb's mother. The two women shared several sad, worry-filled glances, but neither spoke. There didn't seem to be much to say under the dire circumstances.

After a long, restless night in the upright, vinyl-covered chairs and small sofas, everyone began to stir. Dash took Buddy outside before going on a coffee run and returning with dark, steaming brews for each of the adults. Two of Caleb's sisters went to the vending machines in the hallways to secure packs of tiny donuts and cans of juice for the kids. Willow was touched when his oldest sister handed her a ham sandwich, indicating she should give the meat to Buddy.

Just as Willow was debating going up to the desk to demand an update, the surgeon from the night before emerged from the double doors. The woman looked even more exhausted than she had the night before, which made Willow wonder if the doctor had spent the remainder of the night here, too.

The surgeon didn't force them to comply with the socially acceptable morning greetings that would have been polite. Instead, she seemed to know that they were desperate to hear how Caleb was doing, so she dove right in as soon as she was within earshot.

The adults stood anxiously huddled together as the doctor told them that he had made it through the night, but hadn't yet woken up.

"Can we see him?" Cassidy asked, not bothering to hide the desperation in her tone.

The doctor gave her a grim look as she said, "Yes, but keep it brief. No kids or DOGS," she said pointedly before adding, "and immediately family only." The no-nonsense woman told them as she swished back through the doors she had emerged from.

Willow felt extraneous as she watched Caleb's family members prepare to go see him. When one of Caleb's older sisters pointed out that someone needed to stay back to watch the children, Willow immediately offered to help. "I'll keep an eye on them."

"No, you're coming back with us." Cassidy said firmly.

"The doctor said family only," Willow reminded her with a sad smile.

Caleb's mother spoke to Willow for the first time, saying confidently, "Caleb considers you family, and he will want to see you."

When the woman held out her arm towards her, Willow gladly accepted her embrace. She was quickly engulfed into a group hug with the women in Caleb's family. It was the first time in her entire life that she had felt accepted into the folds of a real, loving family, and it was glorious.

Grace volunteered to watch Buddy and the children with Dash, and just like that, Willow was shuffled forward as one of the female members of Caleb's immediate family.

44

*W*illow was stunned by the sight of her big, strong, seemingly-infallible bodyguard resting in a hospital bed. He was connected to all kinds of beeping and medicine-infusing contraptions that made him look vulnerable. She wanted nothing more than for him to open his eyes and proclaim his undying love for her, but he remained motionless.

His mom and sisters circled the bed, leaving a spot for Willow. Willow couldn't help but notice how loving and positive they all were as they talked to him, fussed over him, and teased him about all the babysitting and work they needed him to do as soon as he was better. They acted like he was awake and could hear every word they were saying.

Willow had always longed for a big, warm and welcoming family, but getting this inside glimpse of what it would really be like to be included in one made her realize exactly how much she had been missing. Her aloof mother had occasionally tried to make their house feel like a home, but her constant criticizing and judgmental nature had only managed to make Willow feel even more lonely.

Caleb's mom smoothed a loving hand across his forehead to brush his hair back out of the way. After she leaned down to press a tender kiss to his cheek, she said to her daughters, "We'll let him have a few moments alone with his woman."

Willow shook her head, "Oh, I'm not..."

"Yes," Cassidy interrupted her denial, "You are."

Not wanting to fight with them and wishing that it could be the truth, Willow merely smiled at the ladies as they told Caleb goodbye and filed out of his hospital room. Once his sisters were gone, Caleb's diminutive mother looked up at a Willow and asked, "You love my son?"

Willow felt like she had been put on the spot by this tiny spitfire's unwavering gaze. She thought over the question for a long moment, even though she already knew the answer without the shadow of a doubt. Deciding to go with the truth, she said in a clear voice, "Yes, I do."

Nodding her approval, Caleb's mom patted Willow's cheek on her way out. "Good. Because he loves you, too."

Delighted that Caleb had mentioned her to his mother, but disappointed that the woman had obviously misunderstood his feelings, Willow moved to sit down on the side of Caleb's bed and took his hand within hers.

When he spoke, his voice was so soft and quiet that she almost thought she imagined it. His eyes remained closed, and he didn't move a muscle.

Willow leaned her face in close to his and asked, "Caleb, did you say something? Do you need something? I can call the doctor."

This time when he spoke, his voice was raspy, but louder than a whisper when he said, "You love me?"

Mortification flooded her system that he had heard her admission. She had implied it earlier, but hadn't actually said the words. Pulling back slightly to look at him, she said quietly but seriously, "Yes, I do."

Quickly rushing on, she added, "But it's okay that you don't feel that way about me. I know I'm too old for you and am probably not your type at all."

His eyes were barely more than slits when he said, "Love you, too."

Willow almost couldn't believe her ears. She wanted further confirmation, but his eyes had already drifted shut and his breathing evened out. She wondered if the drugs they were pumping into him were making him delirious, and if he would even remember what they had said once he really woke up.

Deciding he needed his rest, she gently removed her hand from his, preparing to get up and leave. The slight jostling must have been enough to wake him because he croaked the word, "Stay."

That one-word request was all she needed to

hear. She didn't want to get into trouble with his doctors, but a team of sled dogs couldn't have dragged her away from his bedside, if he wanted her there. This was where she belonged, for as long as Caleb needed her––or at least until the pain meds wore off, and he realized that they'd made him loopy enough to say he loved her.

Nurses came in and out to check on Caleb, but no one questioned her right to be at his bedside. She knew she should probably go check on Buddy, but she assumed Grace and Dash could keep him. Star would probably love having a temporary canine sibling.

Caleb slept restlessly, but he didn't have any more lucid moments for the rest of the day. She smiled sadly to herself as she wondered if he had been coherent at all when he proclaimed his love for her. It didn't make sense for him to love her, but she hoped with all her might that it was true.

When darkness fell again, she managed to doze off in the chair beside Caleb's bed. Her head bobbed to the side and she was startled awake. She could see from the glow in the room that Caleb had opened his eyes and was looking at her.

"You're up," she stood to head out to the hall-way. "We should tell your doctors."

"Wait," he ordered her, his voice sounding much stronger than it had before. When he said in a serious tone, "We need to talk," Willow swallowed audibly and sat back down.

Disappointment surged through her as she waited to see what the revelation would be from those four ominous little words. They usually weren't followed by anything good.

Her mouth felt dry, but she tried to keep her tone light when she said, "Okay. What's up?"

"What I said earlier…" He prompted her, which made Willow nod in confirmation that she knew that he was referring to when he said he loved her. "I think you may have misunderstood."

45

*W*illow felt like she might faint. As much as she had tried to convince herself that it was just the drugs flowing through his system that had made Caleb proclaim his love for her, she had allowed a tiny bit of hope to creep in that he had actually meant it.

She chastised herself for stupidly believing that this young, virile man might actually have real romantic feelings for her, rather than the simple, platonic feelings that naturally developed from spending so much time with someone. He was probably only interested in dating firm twenty-something co-eds. What had possessed her to think that he might want to be with a woman who was developing crow's feet and sprouting gray hairs?

Feeling silly for allowing herself to hope, she said, "Oh, I understand. You were doped up on some serious drugs." She flicked her hand in the direction of one of his IV bags that held a clear fluid. "I won't hold you to anything that you said while you were under the influence."

"I am feeling rather loopy." Caleb admitted with a lopsided grin.

Willow couldn't keep the downcast expression off her face, which made Caleb immediately turn serious. "I'm not so loopy that I don't know how I feel, though."

Nodding and trying to hold back her tears, Willow said, "Right... I get it. We've grown to care about each other's well-being––to the point that it could be called love. After all, you did jump in front of a bullet for me. You probably consider me a step or two down from one of your sisters, who are all wonderful, by the way." She tried to give him a brave smile, but feared that it ended up looking more like a grimace.

Looking up at her as she stood over him, Caleb said, "I was afraid your mind would go there. No, that's not how I feel at all."

Horror that she had managed to overestimate his feelings for her again swept over Willow. "Oh," she said as her mouth remained in the shape of the letter for a long moment. "I'm just someone that you've been hired to protect, and you were merely doing your job." Willow nodded her head with grim understanding before going on. "About that... you're fired."

"No. Wait... what?!?" Caleb's expression morphed from one of frustration into a perplexed look.

"They caught the shooter, so the threat has been eliminated."

A look of immense relief swept over Caleb's face before Willow went on. "Besides, my life isn't any more important than yours––or anyone else's. I can't stand idly by while you risk yourself by stepping in front of danger for me."

"I would gladly do that, even if I wasn't working for you," Caleb told her sincerely.

Nodding, Willow said, "Yes, and that is part of what makes you such an incredible human being, but I'm not willing to allow you to take such risks for me any longer. It has been torture waiting and wondering if you were going to be okay. I wouldn't be able to live with myself if you suffered permanent damage trying to protect me."

"I have suffered permanent damage, though."

At Willow's stricken look, Caleb lifted her hand within his to hover an inch over his bandaged chest wound. "Not here," he clarified before placing her hand directly on his heart. "Here."

His heart was thumping wildly. Willow blinked several times as she tried to comprehend exactly what he was trying to tell her.

"I may not be able to express it eloquently, but I'm madly in love with you, Willow Winks."

She shook her head slightly as she tried to absorb his glorious words.

"And before you jump to the wrong conclusion again... My feelings for you aren't of the sibling variety. At all." His voice dropped to a deeper baritone with the last two words, and he wriggled his eyebrows suggestively, effectively eliminating any doubt about his intended meaning.

"Oh, Caleb, I feel the same way about you, but…"

"No buts." He interrupted her.

Feeling stubborn, Willow said adamantly, "BUT we aren't right for each other."

Caleb's brows furrowed into a deep vee before he demanded. "Why not?"

"I'm too old for you." When he started to object, she held up a hand to stop him. "You are so wonderful with kids, and you deserve to be a father, but I am quickly coming to the end of that road. I can't and won't take that opportunity away from you."

"I love my nieces and nephews to pieces, but only in small doses. I have so much fun with them because I am able to send them home to their parents after our adventures. I'm not at all sure I would get the same enjoyment out of it if they were my responsibility all the time."

Willow shook her head, not believing him for a second. "You're just saying that because you think it's what I want to hear. You were made to be a dad."

"Have you ruled out the possibility of becoming a mother? You shouldn't--you are absolutely amazing with Buddy."

Willow smiled as she thought of her wonderful bond with Buddy. "No, I haven't decided against it. I just don't think I'm ready right now, and I don't want to limit your available options."

"I'm not ready right now, either. What I am certain of is that I want to be with you. If we both decide down the road that we are ready to be parents--to human children, in addition to our sweet dog--we can explore our options at that time."

Willow couldn't quite comprehend his wonderful words. They were more than she would have dared to hope for. Needing to verify, she asked him, "Are you sure?"

Smiling confidently, Caleb said, "I've never been more sure about anything. I want to spend the rest of my life loving you."

"I can't imagine a better future."

"Even though our astrological signs don't align well?" Caleb teased her.

"I'm willing to take my chances," Willow smiled before leaning down to press a gentle kiss to his cheek.

Caleb surprised her by turning his head quickly so her lips landed on his. Pulling back and slowly opening her eyes, Willow said dreamily, "I do have one confession to make before we move together into our happily ever after."

"Yeah?" Caleb's brows rose up towards his hairline. "What's that?"

Willow swallowed nervously, knowing she needed to confess her lie. Looking away and tucking a stray lock of hair behind her ear, she finally admitted, "I'm not really 37."

Caleb smiled at her with a mischievous look sparkling in his eyes. He leaned up towards her and whispered, "That's okay because I'm not really 27."

"What?!?" Willow screeched. "You're not younger than that, are you??"

Caleb's delighted laughter echoed down the hospital halls as Willow grinned down at him and realized that their ages didn't really matter at all. Their matchmaking dog had selected them as a perfectly imperfect couple, and she had a feeling they were destined to be just that.

The day was finally here. Willow didn't feel nearly as nervous as she had expected she would as she gazed at the reflection of the beautiful bride in the mirror.

Her sleek, sophisticated, white, crystal-beaded gown from Hidden Gem bridal shop, a local boutique, was the perfect picture of understated elegance. The hair and makeup team from the show had worked on her for over an hour, but she had asked them not to overdo it.

The resulting overall look of the bride gazing back at her was stunning––mostly because of the aura of pure happiness emanating out from deep within her.

"I always said happy girls are the prettiest." Her mother's raspy voice startled her from the doorway.

"Mother, it's nice to see you," Willow greeted her formally as she waited for the expected critical follow-up to her mother's entrance. The standoffish woman only ever gave Willow backhanded compliments that left her feeling worse than before. When no jabs came, Willow turned and opened her arms towards her mother.

After a stiff hug, her mother awkwardly patted Willow on the back and pulled away. "I'm so happy you've finally found someone to marry you."

The dig was nothing less than she had been expecting, so Willow made an attempt to be gracious. "I'm very lucky because he's a wonderful man, and we are deeply in love."

"That's lovely." Her mother gave her a brittle smile.

Willow was relieved when the knock rapped on the doorframe. "Come in," she offered, already feeling grateful to whoever was on the other side.

Her Matron of Honor, Grace, and her brides-maids, who were also soon to be her sisters-in-law, scurried in. After many hugs and exclamations over what a lovely bride she was, the group formed a natural circle around her.

Willow had almost forgotten her mother was still in the room, until the woman loudly cleared her throat to get their attention. "Well, I guess I'll be going, then."

"You can stay," Cassidy offered kindly, but she stopped abruptly when she saw that Willow's mother's mouth was puckered in distaste and her arms were crossed tightly over her chest. The woman couldn't have made it clearer that she was uncomfortable and wished to leave, unless she had announced it with a megaphone.

"I need to find my seat." She was already

backing out of the room as she uttered the flimsy excuse.

"Goodbye, mother," Willow said, determined not to let the bristly, judgmental woman put a damper on her big day.

Once the door was closed behind her, Cassidy said, "Wow, she's not exactly maternal, is she?"

"No," Willow shook her head, before adding, "But that's okay because I have plenty of wonderful and supportive women in my life now." She beamed a wide smile as she was engulfed into a group hug with Grace and Caleb's sisters.

"We're not just in your life," Caleb's oldest sister informed her. "We're your family now."

Just when Willow had started to believe that she couldn't possibly be any happier, she was proven wrong. She couldn't have imagined how amazing it would feel to have the loving support and friendship that these women provided. She spent a long moment basking in their warm embrace.

Cassidy broke the silence by saying, "Although I'm appalled that you are for some strange reason physically attracted to my brother," she shivered with mock disgust to emphasize her point, "I'm thrilled that you two found each other."

Nods and murmurs of agreement ensued. Once that died down, Cassidy kicked them into gear by saying, "Let's do this!"

The wedding planner and her assistants stood at the entrance to the church's sanctuary. As Caleb's sisters and Grace passed by, they were each handed an adorable, adoptable shelter puppy to carry down the aisle.

The puppies had collars made of fresh flowers, which served as each woman's bouquet. The effect was stunning as the women walked down the aisle and met at the altar.

As the string quartet began playing The Bridal Chorus, Caleb's nieces and nephews made their way down the aisle with Buddy, who proudly carried a drawstring bag containing the rings. His tail wagged with excitement. It appeared that the natural showman sensed that he was playing a vital role in a momentous occasion.

Caleb bent down to greet the happy animal. Buddy tried to lick the groom, which made the guests titter. When Willow faintly heard Caleb good-naturedly tell the dog to keep his smoocher to himself, she couldn't even imagine loving either of the handsome males in her life any more than she already did.

When the instruments upped the volume at the chorus of "Here Comes the Bride" everyone stood and turned to face the back of the cathedral. Dash had his arm looped around Willow's elbow as he remained steady by her side. He let her take charge as she paused at the threshold to absorb the significance of this moment.

Taking a deep breath, Willow stepped forward to begin her walk down the aisle. Dash effortlessly stayed in sync with the pace Willow set. As soon as Willow locked eyes with her groom, her pre-wedding jitters dissipated. The love-filled, adoring gaze he was giving her was even better than she had imagined it could be.

Once the ceremony started, it went by in a marvelous, but too fast, blur. Before she knew what had happened, Willow was married to the man of her dreams. She felt as if she was floating on a cloud as she circulated and spoke to her guests at their wedding reception.

When Caleb presented her with a small, foil-wrapped present, she worried over the fact that she hadn't gotten him anything. "You're all the gift I need," he assured her before adding, "Besides, it isn't much."

She looked at him uncertainly, so he encouraged her, "Open it."

Unable to hide the excitement in her eyes as she ripped the package open, she wondered what he could have gotten her. Recognition flickered in her mind as she pulled the ceramic mug out of the box. It looked like the one she had broken in Caleb's room, but it was decorated with intricate gold lines. Uncertain what she was looking at, she turned a questioning gaze up at Caleb.

"I fixed your favorite mug with the ancient art of Kintsugi, which roughly translates to golden joinery. In Japan, broken pottery is often repaired in this manner. The gold lines are not seen as flaws, but as unique reminders of the object's history, which add to its beauty. My goal as your husband will be to help you remember this whenever you feel broken."

Willow couldn't believe how marvelous his words and sentiment were. He seemed to have an innate sense of knowing exactly what she needed to hear. A single tear of happiness meandered down her cheek. Caleb gave her an earnest look as he gently swiped it away with the back of his finger.

Not sensing the intimacy of the moment, Mandy ran up to give Willow a tight hug. Joe stood silently by his wife's side. "Everything was lovely," Mandy practically gushed before adding, "And those puppies were absolutely adorable. That was such a nice touch."

"That was Caleb's idea." Willow beamed at her husband as she gave him credit. "We've been volunteering at the local animal shelter, and he thought it might be a nice way to help some of them get adopted."

"It worked, too." Caleb informed them. "The volunteer coordinator told me a little bit ago that all of the puppies have been adopted."

"That's fantastic!" Willow set down her beautifully repaired mug and lifted up a champagne glass to toast with the others. Just when she started to think she couldn't possibly be any happier, her new husband found a way to make it happen.

When the romantic song, "A Thousand Years," began playing, Caleb whisked his bride out onto the dance floor. She was delighted to see that the lessons they had been taking for months were paying off so well. Her groom was a fluid and graceful dancer.

Concerned about all of the activity, she lightly placed her flat palm over his injured chest. "You aren't overdoing it, are you?"

"It's nothing I can't handle," he promised her.

She could feel her brows furrowing together as she worried that he might be pushing himself too hard to make sure she had a perfect day. Caleb gently pressed his lips to the line between her brows before trailing kisses down the slope of her nose and finally landing on her lips.

When their kiss lingered, Willow finally forced herself to pull back. Several people clapped at the newlywed couple's public display of affection as Caleb dipped his head down for another kiss.

Feeling self-conscious, since she wasn't used to publicly sharing such an intimate side of herself, Willow pulled back slightly and said, "Everyone is watching us."

"Are there other people here?" Caleb asked innocently before adding, "I hadn't noticed."

Willow laughed at her silly, sweet husband before saying with an ornery gleam in her eye, "Let's go have a piece of our peach-infused wedding cake."

"Peach wedding cake??" Caleb wrinkled his nose in distaste. "You're kidding, right?!?"

Willow answered him with a joyous laugh, filled to the brim with pure happiness.

Curious about Dash Diamond and his golden co-host, Star? Read their story, *Guarding Grace* (Gold Coast Retrievers, Book 3). Available NOW!

If you've enjoyed the Gold Coast Retrievers books and want more sweet romance (plus puppies), curl up with the charming and heartwarming novella, *Goofy Newfies*.

MORE SWEET ROMANCE
FEATURING LOVABLE DOGS

Be sure to read *Goofy Newfies*, the sweet romance inspired by Rocky & Cheerio (The big, loving, and goofy Newfies who claimed me as their human).

REVIEWS ~ BEST. GIFT. EVER.

Now is the time to help other readers. Many people rely on reviews to make the decision about whether or not to buy a book. You can help them make that decision by leaving your thoughts on what you found enjoyable about this book.

If you liked this book, please consider leaving a positive review. Even if it's just a few words, your input makes a difference and will be received with much gratitude.

LET'S STAY IN TOUCH!

Join Ann Omasta's Reader Group:

Get VIP access. Be the first to know about new releases, sales, freebies, and exclusive giveaways. We value your privacy and will not send spam. Join at annomasta.com!

COPYRIGHT

Watching Willow ~ The Gold Coast Retrievers
   Copyright: Ann Omasta
   Published: January 2019
   All rights reserved.

Cheerio loves helping me write:

Made in the USA
Las Vegas, NV
14 January 2022

41418622R00157